An Unexpected Gift

KJ

2020

An Unexpected Gift © 2020 By KJ. All Rights Reserved.
This Electronic Original Is Self-Published.
First Edition: November 2020
This is a work of fiction. Names, characters, places, and incidents are the product of the author's imagination or are used fictitiously. Any resemblance to actual persons, living or dead, business establishments, events, or locales is entirely coincidental. This book, or parts thereof, may not be reproduced in any form without permission.

Acknowledgements

Christmas in Australia is such a strange phenomenon for those in the northern hemisphere. The concept of searing heat, cricket on the sand, wrapping paper sticking to sweaty skin, and cold cuts of meat with salad for Christmas lunch and dinner, is unbelievably foreign for those used to snow, mulled wine, and beanies. Therefore, I wanted to share with readers a snapshot of an Australian Christmas on one street in a Melbourne beachside suburb during the week leading up to December 25. I hope you enjoy this collection about the daily unexpected gifts that life delivers, but especially those we receive at Christmas.

Thank you to Sophie L, Fiona Mc, AC, and Em. You're all wonderful people.

I acknowledge the assistance I received from members of the South Sudanese Community in crafting a true representation of South Sudanese culture and customs for the story 'Finding Faith'

I sincerely hope you enjoy reading *An Unexpected Gift*. If you do, I would greatly appreciate a review on your favourite book website. Or even a recommendation in your favourite lesbian fiction Facebook group. Reviews and recommendations are crucial for any author, and even just a line or two can make a huge difference. Thanks!

About the author

Best-selling author KJ lives in Melbourne, Australia with her wife, their son, three cats and a dog. Her novel, Coming Home, was a Goldie finalist. Her other best-selling novels include Learning To Swim, Kick Back, and Art of Magic.

Twitter at @propertyofkj
Instagram at kjlesfic
Facebook at https://www.facebook.com/kj.lesfic.7/
Subscribe to my newsletter
https://tinyletter.com/KJauthor

Dedication

For Roanne
My unexpected gift

Christmas Angel

I like where I work. At the *BargainBuy* supermarket on Wilkins Street with the tramline at one end and Laskin Beach down the other. That beach is a major tourist drawcard. The Council threw money at it last year and a massive fancy-pants lifeguard tower appeared over the winter and spring, just in time for the hordes of people who swell the population of our sleepy Melbourne suburb during the Christmas summer holidays. My job is pretty straightforward. Sure, there are times when the day's road changes direction entirely and heads out cross-country through the bush and crashes into the trees. Every job has those days.

Mind you, I'm one of the most invisible people in society. Except when something doesn't go someone's way. Then I may as well wear a neon sign, rather than my pressed black pants and green and yellow-checked shirt. At the moment, head office has insisted that we all wear plastic holly pins on our collars to, and I quote, "brighten the customer's day" which means that when I'm visible to a frustrated customer at Christmas, I'm very visible. Christmas is a great season. I love it. But sometimes Christmas can be the worst.

"This was marked down to one dollar forty, and you rang it up as two dollars."

The man, maybe in his sixties but it's hard to tell under the flat golfer's cap, glares at me. He dumps the packet of biscuits, which will now be crushed, onto the counter of my checkout, and leans forward. Perhaps he wants to intimidate me. Who knows. People generally say that they're more intimidated *by* me, not the other way around. Sure, I'm tall. And broad-shouldered. And I'm not in the sort of shape I was five years ago when I was hurling javelins for medals. Not quite. Cycling to work keeps my twenty-eight-year-old body going, even with the few spongy bits. I surreptitiously poke my stomach. Spongy. Doesn't matter. I like that my pants fit and I'm happy with my shape. But I don't think I'm intimidating. The opposite actually. I'm as shy as a pastel at a party for primary colours.

"I want to see the manager," Golfer Hat demands. I smile politely.

"Well, that's me. If I could have your receipt, then we'll look at getting this item refunded and a new packet of biscuits to replace these." I smile again. "Just in case they're broken."

He goggles. "Well…yes. Fine." He reaches into his shopping bag —the green ones that the supermarket sells—and fishes out a receipt. I take it from his fingers, and he goes back to studying me. I know I confuse him. I confuse a few people. In their minds, the tall, broad-shouldered situation combined with my short haircut that some consider 'manly' doesn't work with my soft voice and my name, which they can read on the tag pinned to my shirt. They also don't expect a manager to be working one of the registers. Perhaps they're alarmed by plastic holly.

With the money in his hand, a new pack of biscuits in his bag, and my sincere apology tucked into his ears, I wish Golfer Hat a great day and a Merry Christmas. I'm even fine with only receiving a mumbled version in reply. I expect it, and really, who wants to hear a million 'Merry Christmas' wishes every day this close to the actual date? Just meaningless. So I settle back into being an invisible person behind one of the ten checkouts at the front of *BargainBuy*.

Christmas should be lovely this year. I'm going to visit Mum, and my sister will be there with her three kids and coleslaw. I'll take a few of the Christmas puddings and the cakes that I can get the staff discount on. Maybe a pavlova. That'll go down well, seeing as it's an Australian dessert. Mum's a bit nationalistic about her sweets.

I spend the next hour scanning people's items, handing out trolley tokens for the folk who don't have a dollar coin, running through a couple more refunds—must get the price-fix guys to sort out the shelf markers—and giving directions to the toilets and the aisle with the aluminium foil—two different places. All the while wishing folk a merry or happy or have-a-great Christmas, and adjusting the tinsel taped to the front of the counters, so it doesn't get sucked down the end of the conveyor belt to jam up the machinery.

I'm leaning into the register, halfway through my once-a-week five-hour shift operating register eight, when it occurs to me. Again. The front-end area is a study in human nature, observing customers interacting—or not—with service staff. Take tall, blonde, yoga woman—organic cereal, almond milk, and the bunch of kale leading the charge along the conveyor belt—who's a regular customer on Tuesdays, and currently going through register seven. She barely acknowledged Kevin's greeting. She's staring into space, past his right shoulder as he scans the six-pack of coconut water and places it at the bottom of the bag so light stuff can go on top—good job, Kev. I guess her head is full of thoughts and having to make conversation with an eighteen-year-old university student in the week leading to Christmas was never going to be a priority.

See? Invisible.

Unlike my blue-eyed angel. She sees me.

A number of weeks ago, a collection of items building a cityscape at the end of my conveyor belt jolted me from my philosophical reverie. I activated the belt, and tossed out my familiar "how are you today?" so it travelled all the way to the end. My hand landed on the first item—one of three onions—and I looked up and over the produce to the trolley parked at the other end. The onion slipped a little in my grip as I fell into the bluest pair of eyes I'd ever seen. A gorgeous smile stretched the lips underneath and they moved to give the reply. "Great, thanks."

I yanked my head down and focused on scanning. Beep. The automatic movements settled my ridiculous nerves that always appeared whenever my shyness was activated. Beep. Swap hands. Place item into bag. Beep. Then—

"How's your morning been, Emily?" I froze, my fist clutching the bag of apples which was swaying softly in the air as their journey to the red laser screen was dramatically cut short. I looked up. Wow. Dimples, which I hadn't noticed before, pushed into her cheeks. Light brown hair, like cinnamon, framed a beautiful round face. Her dark purple blouse showcased her curves. Curves in wonderful places. And a couple of extra curves, just for good measure. An extravagant delight. And then I realised she'd said my name. Customers don't say my name, despite my obvious name tag. It's probably a protective mannerism. If they don't use my name, even if they've read it, then they haven't engaged with me and therefore are free to leave any conversation at any given moment, reload their trolley, and carry on with their day. Names create tension. Names render people visible.

I cleared my throat.

"It's been good. Thank you," I said softly, and the skin around her eyes crinkled as she happily absorbed my response. Thank goodness for muscle memory, because my hands carried on scanning and packing when they realised my brain had fallen out of the car and was staring blankly at the sky from the side of the road. She beamed, and dropped her head to fossick around in her purse. She was my age. Maybe. It's hard to tell sometimes. I wanted to say something so that more dialogue continued and therefore it qualified as a conversation. But as I whisked her twin-tub of vanilla yoghurt—the final item sitting starkly on the black belt—into her cooler bag and zipped it up, I realised I'd lost my chance.

"Uh. That's seventy-four dollars, please," I stated automatically. I pressed the amount into the keypad and she swiped her card, the plastic rectangle pressed delicately between her thumb and the curve of her index finger. Her hand looked like it could smooth a brow. Like it would hold a porcelain cup. She smelled like fresh flowers.

She smiled into my eyes, her hair falling in waves to her shoulders, then she lifted the last bag into her trolley. There were only four bags. It was the shopping expedition of a single person buying seven day's worth of groceries. Perhaps she'd be back next week. Perhaps this wasn't her regular supermarket. Perhaps she was visiting someone.

"Have a great day, Emily."

I gave a start, then I returned her smile. Mine was shy. "You too."

I watched her leave, pushing hard with the left side of her body to counteract the wonky wheel on the right at the front of the trolley. The action pulled the material of her black capri pants across the roundness of her bum, and my tummy flipped over.

***

"Excuse me."

The voice, abrupt, like I've been caught smoking behind the bike sheds in the school grounds, explodes my little daydream cloud. I whip my head back to respond to the new customer, who's glaring at me through glasses that have those little wingtips at the sides of the frames. I didn't think anyone wore that style in this decade and the thought makes me smile. Luckily, she thinks the gesture is for her, because she flaps her hand at the jumble of items on my conveyor belt and responds with a fairly amenable "hmmph" when I ask her how she is today and what she'll be up to for Christmas on Saturday. I rearrange my face into customer-service-Emily, rather than remembering-gorgeous-woman-Emily.

I'm packing away her cereal—oats, bran, shredded cardboard mix —when she frowns at me. A specific frown aimed at my head.

"I'd have said something to the hairdresser, if it was me."

I blink, and she tosses her finger at my hair. "I hope you didn't have to pay," she elaborates. I slid my free hand over the short sides above my ear, feeling the upright strands bristling under my fingertips. I blush softly. I know I'm not a fashion-plate or probably much to look at, but I'm spick 'n span and my smile reaches my eyes. Not now, though. My scanning-to-packing pace picks up slightly and within a minute, I'm wishing her a good day and a "M'Christmas".

She grasps the handle of her trolley and delivers a nod and a stiff smile—I've been flicked back to the 'nice' list—and flaps her hand at my hair. All loose wrist and circular motion.

"The good thing about hair is that it grows back."

She heads off, steering her trolley of grocery trophies, including the last tin of Danish shortbread biscuits from aisle seven, across the slick tiles in the forecourt, and out into the stinking heat of the carpark. I take a deep breath. The hierarchical imbalance has been maintained. Personal comments—including opinions about hair—are par for the course, but only if the customer delivers them. I couldn't imagine making a similar comment to a customer. My inbox would explode with requests from head office to "fucking explain myself".

***

My face softens as I remember the second time my blue-eyed angel visited me. Jonno and I had just fist-bumped when I'd replaced him at register eight the following week. I smile quietly. I don't generally think of myself as a fist-bumping sort, but hiring teenagers and early twenty-somethings has increased exponentially my repertoire of hand-head-finger gestures. That day, I turned slowly in my little space behind the register, looking up and down the checkouts. Everything looked good. Plastic Christmas decorations were creeping into the store, dangling from the metal strips holding the square ceiling tiles in place. There were enough cheesy Santas to make folk aware of the impending consumerism that was about to descend upon them. Various wandering customers were happy, despite wearing the 'fluorescent-lighting-is-eating-my-soul' expression that Kaz came up with a year ago at our staff meeting. I nodded in satisfaction, checked my watch—ten-fifteen—wriggled my shoulders, and look down the end of the conveyor belt. Straight into the blue eyes of the mystery woman from the previous week. I'm pretty sure I blinked for a long moment before my training kicked in.

"How are you today?"

The woman, again dressed in capris but this time topped with a pale blue shirt which looked so soft that my fingers itched to touch it, smiled, resting her gaze on mine as she put her last item—a loaf of bread—on the end. She wheeled her trolley through, turned to me, and held onto the edge of the counter.

"I'm really well, Emily. How about you?"

It was a delightful voice. A delightful voice that said my name.

Muscle memory. Muscle memory. Pick up. Scan. Pack. Repeat.

"I'm well. Thanks." I waited for my brain to take charge of its steering wheel. "Are you having a busy day today?" Brilliant.

The woman tipped her head from side-to-side, her hair shuffling slightly with the movement so that she had to flip it away when she stopped. "Somewhat. Christmas is coming up soon, and Tuesdays are my day off, so I tend to fill it with chores and a bit of running around." She beamed, like I'd asked her to share something joyous. It was intoxicating. I blinked, realised I was about to scan her last item, and felt instantly bereft. The loaf of bread travelled towards the bag.

"I'm on this checkout on Tuesdays," I blurted. I may as well have taken out advertising space on a billboard to announce my interest. I could feel the tension of embarrassment seeping into my neck muscles. The woman paused to look at me. Properly look at me, like she enjoyed what she saw. Then she smiled again, tapped her card, and grabbed hold of the trolley bar.

"Sounds like we both have busy Tuesdays. See you next time, Emily," she said, and she walked away, delicious hips swaying. I wrenched my eyes back to my watch. Ten-twenty. Five minutes. Okay. I'd make them count next time.

***

They say Christmas brings out the best and worst in some people, but I'm positive some people are either one or the other all year-round. Sasha reckons she occasionally serves a guy who says nothing at all and looks right through her like she's transparent when she asks how he is. She's convinced he's a serial killer, and got so worked up about him one time that I had to send her to fruit and veg to rearrange pineapples just to calm her down.

The middle-aged white man standing in front of me in his ill-fitting business shirt is probably one of those year-round people. He's on his phone. There's a lot of "uh-huh" and "no, I told her" and "forward me the emails" and "I'll see you at the staff party tonight" going on. He's buying boxes of *BargainBuy*'s own brand tea biscuits —probably for the staff party—which are the exact same consistency as roof insulation. I wonder why he's buying them and not a junior staff member, because he seems to hold a level of importance in his company if his phone conversation is anything to go by. I bet he doesn't see people as individuals. Not like my gorgeous mystery Tuesday Goddess. I wonder what she does for work? I bet she's incredibly important, like folks depend on her. I bet she'd buy the fancy biscuits for their staff party.

I have a habit of falling into these moments of analysis. It is so unnecessary. Like analysing why I'm crushing on a customer, even though she's only been through my checkout a couple of times. The only possible reason is because she says my name, which is bullshit. I load more biscuit packets into a bag. Mystery woman says my name which makes me gooey, and she is beautiful and seems so lovely, and I've had ten minutes of vacuous conversation with her so I have no idea what I'm talking about. Business-suit guy checks his green bags, peering at each one like the Queen inspecting the troops. It is all too tempting to lean over and whack my fist into the centre of the top packets just to see his reaction, which wouldn't be great role-modelling for my front-end crew.

"Forty dollars fifty, please."

His card, the fancy matte black type, flops onto the screen and then he's gone, probably to check on those emails.

***

I think back to last Tuesday and the most recent visit from my blue-eyed angel.

"Hi Emily. How's your day going?"

My smile started before I even lifted my head, and I sent the smile down the end of the belt. It was her. She loaded the final item.

"It's going well. Thank you." I held her gaze as she came to a halt in front of me, the display screen perched between us like an annoying cinema-goer in the seat in front. I shuffled slightly so we could see each other more clearly and I started her scan-through.

"You jumped in before I could," I said. It was pretty much the most inarticulate sentence I'd ever uttered, but she seemed to understand because she laughed.

"Go ahead, then."

I paused. "How are you today?"

She bit her lip, and the LED numbers on my screen got nice and fuzzy.

"I'm actually really well. I had a breakthrough with a client yesterday and I'm totally celebrating." She grinned and pointed to the chocolate bar that I was sending through to its final destination. I quickly calculated the items remaining with the average amount of time a half-belt load of groceries took to process. I had about two minutes left.

"Celebration chocolate. I like the sound of that." Scan. Pack. Grin. Gosh, that blue is amazing.

"Oh, it's essential." She lifted her eyebrows. "Small wins should be celebrated."

I nodded. Then I stared at the insistent flashing screen, which was announcing the end of another five-minute date.

She looked back at me just before she exited through the automatic doors.

***

I want her to visit today, being Tuesday and all, but I figure that because it's so close to Christmas, she won't. But that would be a perfect early present.

"What do you reckon we'll get to on Saturday?"

I'm scanning the tenth of fourteen cans of dog food for the old bloke who has a German Shepherd and buys the cheapest food we sell. His house must stink of farts and wet fur. I figure his question is about the weather, which a few of us get asked quite a lot. I'm not sure why. Perhaps we're the first people they've seen in their day and they're hoping that we'll know because we've been out of our houses longer.

"Looks like it'll be another hot one. Good for a beer under the air-con and maybe a mince pie to celebrate." I zip up his cooler bag. "That's sixty-one twenty, please."

He pays. "Thanks, luv." He shoves on the trolley bar, hunching his shoulders and leaning forward like he's supporting the back row of a rugby rolling maul. 'Luv' and 'hon' are quite common for nearly all the front-end staff. I tend to get 'mate' a lot. It's a handy inoffensive label that covers any potentially awkward situation for a customer who's used to delivering a term of endearment as part of their vocabulary.

My checkout is clear of customers, which is an unexpected gift as people tend to shop at Christmas like a plague is arriving and they need to buy all the stock in case they never get to leave their house again. Then I catch a flash of red rounding the corner of aisle five which is in a direct line to my conveyor belt. It's her. In a red shirt and Santa hat. She's making her way towards me, but another trolley suddenly appears and pushes up to the metal bar at the end. The young mum, with her toddler, his limbs shoved through strategic holes in the seat under the handle of the trolley, begins to unload the paraphernalia of parenting. I catch the eye of my mystery woman and smile, receiving a grin in return, a resigned shrug, and an air-hand-pat to indicate that she'll wait. Jubilant at catching an extra few seconds beyond our standard five minutes, I ask how young mum's day is going. She says it's fine, then her glance encompasses my eyes, face, and the surrounding checkout, so I'm not sure I believe her. 'Fine' covers many situations. While I'm scanning through a thousand sachets of baby mush, and the twenty-something-year-old mum is disentangling her hair from the clutches of her toddler, I sneak a glance down the end of the conveyor belt. My stealth is rewarded because she's flicking at her phone screen, completely unaware that I'm fascinated by the way her lips quirk when she sees something amusing. Then I'm caught. Her gaze grabs mine, her lips actually quirk like I'm the amusing something, and I give myself whiplash as I look back at the mum and announce the total.

"How are you today, Emily?"

I smile. A big, genuine, probably goofy kind of smile. Our five minutes have started.

"I'm good, thanks," I say, and send through one of ten boxes of tissues, which confuses me. "Everyone got colds in your house?"

She looks at the Lego stack of boxes still to scan, and laughs. It's wonderful.

"No. It's just me at home. Actually, those are for a couple of my clients. They're elderly and I take essentials when I visit for their physical therapy sessions. Their pensions don't quite go far enough." She gazes up at me, her eyes sad, and suddenly the grocery items refuse to leap into my hands. There's a moment, and time gets a little stretchy, and I want to tell her I think she's marvellous.

"So what was the win last week that caused celebration chocolate?" Scan, pack, scan, pack, scan.

She beams, lifts off her Santa hat, and slides her fingers through her fringe to push it away from her face. "Oh. That's right!" Her eyes crinkle at me, as she pulls the hat back into place. "One of my longterm patients broke his foot a while ago, and he's such a stubborn bugger, but I got him to go for a walk around the retirement village gardens with his walking frame."

"That's great," I say, and I know my smile can't help but be my best. Eyes totally involved. Guaranteed. She seems to like it, because her cheeks pink a little. Scan, pack, scan, pack. The conveyor belt is emptying. There's maybe a minute left.

Then she says, "Just as well I don't have too many unexpected wins. I don't need that much chocolate with the diet I'm starting." She gestures vaguely to her hips, which means I gaze at her curves. And my brain disconnects.

"Why are you dieting?"

She shrugs slightly, searches in her bag for her credit card, and mutters into the void. "The same reason we all do. To look better." Her head pops up, and I press the total button on the keypad.

"That's ninety-six dollars and seventy-five cents."

She presses her card against the little screen, the register spits out the receipt, and as I hand it to her, our fingertips touch and our eyes connect.

"I hope it's okay to say this, but you don't need to diet. You're perfect," I say in the shyest voice I have, and I think both of us are stunned. She blinks, and tips her head, then blushes.

"Thank you, Emily," she says, then she drops her gaze for a moment, before lifting it to meet my eyes. "Have a lovely Christmas," she murmurs, through a soft smile, and with another head tip, she slowly walks away from my register.

Meanwhile, I'm holding the vinyl counter where the black rubber of the belt meets the metal edging and wondering what on earth just happened. Did I actually flirt with a customer? Did she like it? Am I insane? And here's the other part of that hierarchical imbalance that I was talking about. I can't ask for her name. That's not how it works. My name is right there on my shirt for everyone to see and generally ignore. That amazing woman chooses to use my name because she can. But her name is not visible, and it's not my place to ask. That's simply how the transaction works. Visibility for the invisible, and invisibility for the visible.

No new customers are at my register, so I stare out of the store, out into the forecourt with its kitschy decorations and giant reindeer which are stupid because we live in Australia, out in the direction that she's gone. Out, and into her eyes, because she's stopped in the centre next to the enormous fake tree, looking back at me, with people moving around her and the trolley she's clutching, like water around a rock. Both of us are waiting.

I come to a decision. I grab the plastic A-frame 'checkout closed' marker and frisbee it down to the end of my belt, like a skilled bartender sending a drink to a patron. I duck around the side of the checkout, and double-tap Kevin's counter.

"Taking a break, Kev." He shrugs and waves at me, utilising a complicated hand gesture to let me know he's heard.

I'm desperate to move casually. Stroll, even. Strut. No, probably not strut. But I'm walking like one of those Olympic race walkers who's forgotten their technique and is just legging it to the finish line.

She's right here in front of me, my blue-eyed angel. All gorgeous curves, and cinnamon hair, and her beautiful face, and a smile that reaches her eyes, which are looking at me in confusion and hope and nervous energy.

"Hi," I say, then like a stiff breeze whisking the leaves about, my next thought flies away entirely.

Her mouth lifts up at the edges. "Hi."

"Ah." I chew my bottom lip. "So, obviously not this week, because Christmas and all that, but maybe after, I was wondering if you'd like to go on a date? With me? Dinner or something?"

Her mouth curves up further. God, so delightful. "I'd love to, Emily. Perhaps a date that's longer than five minutes?"

I blink, then huff a tiny nervous cough through my lips. She's been having five-minute dates as well. Wow. Now we have matching smiles, and the people continue to flow around us. I shove my left hand into my pocket and pluck out my phone, ready for a new contact. Then it hits me.

I wince and wrinkle my eyebrows.

"I'm so sorry. I don't even know your name." I breathe deeply and stick out my hand. "Hi, my name's Emily."

She giggles, her eyes sparkling with happiness, then the softest of skin slides against my palm.

"Hi Emily. I'm Fiona."

"Fiona," I say, still holding her hand, and relishing the feel of her name in my mouth.

Her smile involves her entire face, then she says, "I think today might actually be Christmas, because I've been waiting so long for you to say my name."

Fiona, my blue-eyed angel.

Unwrap me

The largest of my three art folios slides into the back of my beat-up sedan. It's a deep blue, which I think is a great colour for a 1993 Toyota Corolla. Not a great colour for summer, however, because it retains the heat and transports the interior—with me in it—straight to the middle of the Outback. I give the door a little double-tug. It always needs that second one to disengage from the rest of the car body, then I slide into the cloth-covered seat. I recall my step-dad's face when he first laid eyes on my car. His top lip nearly rolled into his right nostril.

But, today is going to be a good day. I can feel it. Saturday is Christmas Day, which means I have today, tomorrow and Friday to sell all my paintings and prints. I reckon I can. The crowds have been excellent this year, and the Council, well, they've been a revelation. So supportive of the beachside market, with reduced stall-holder fees, and trestle tables and three metre by three metre sunshade tents supplied for each vendor.

I think about Christmas Eve. I'm expected to be home by six o'clock for Mum and Ian, my step-dad, to present me to the rest of the family and other assorted influential people. People who can support Ian's re-election platform. Christianity will save us, and all that. The sanctimony bubbles to the surface around religious holidays, like Christmas. As far as my parents are concerned, Christmas is about the best cutlery, the best clothing, the best smiles, and presenting the best summary of our Christian lives since last December. A walking, talking Facebook feed. It won't be subtle.

"Alexandria! Oh, look. Alexandria is here, everyone. How wonderful," he will boom.

It won't be wonderful. It'll be awkward, and disappointing, and uncomfortable. Mum will ask after my art.

"How is your hobby going? The little paintings?"

As if she doesn't know that I have access to a studio at a friend's place and that I paint on weekends. She knows perfectly well that my art is vivid, and breathes, and is larger than my heart. So her jab is to ensure everyone else understands the need to trivialise that aspect of my life. I can't tell her yet that painting is my whole life and that secretly operating my own stall at the markets is the first step in coming out. To free myself from the restrictions currently in place. I mean coming out as a full-time painter, not closet coming out. Oh, God! I can't do that one yet. I'm only gathering the courage to tell them about the market stall.

Christmas Eve will then continue with my step-dad inquiring about my week-day work. I live with my parents. They know the answers to these questions. It is all for the audience in the sitting room.

"Did you know Alexandria has decided to help out at that little refugee place for three months while she decides on the direction for her law career?" he'll say. He'll nod proudly like he did last month at dinner when I told them what I was doing for the three months after I finished my law degree. Apparently, having a daughter providing free legal assistance to asylum seekers at the largest refugee centre in Melbourne adds extra shine to a politician campaigning on a platform of charity and goodness. Even if they don't like refugees.

Of course, the various cousins, second cousins, Mum's two sisters and their husbands, and the important people will nod and gasp and congratulate, while I try to explain that I prefer to be called Alex. While I try to explain that my work with refugees isn't little but vastly important, and that my paintings are actually, really good and that last year I donated one to a fundraiser, and it fetched three-thousand dollars. While I try to explain that I don't want to use my degree to work for my step-dad's friends because I'd rather poke kale in my eye and this is why I refuse to accept money from my family and why I bought a shitty car with money I'd earned from my paintings. But I won't get to finish that explanation because Mum will jump in and ask everyone if they're interested in hors d'oeuvres.

I caress the seatbelt from its locking mechanism. If I pull too quickly, it jams and I have to talk to it soothingly to get it to release.

Even safety equipment in my car needs help to come out. But I'm clicked in and driving. My journey takes me through quiet suburbs, and I turn into Wilkins Street, juddering over the tram lines. It's early yet, and the *BargainBuy* supermarket carpark has welcomed the staff cars and maybe a couple of eager customers hoping to snag the last of their Christmas groceries. I grin.

Yesterday, I'd raced up to *Bargain Buy* to grab something for lunch, pleading with Soma, the stall-holder next to me who makes exquisite beaded jewellery, to look after my stall. She'd laughed and flapped her hand at me to get going. We watch each other's stuff all the time. It's the market way. With my sandwich and lemonade in hand, I'd walked past a softly awkward scene between the shy butch store manager and a stunning full-figured woman, who I assumed was a customer since she was attached to a laden trolley. I immediately wanted to paint her. They were so wrapped up in each other's eyes and smiles that a naked Santa could have rappelled down through the ceiling and sung 'Oh, Holy Night' into a karaoke machine and they wouldn't have known. I didn't catch what they were saying, but everything about them said 'new' and 'fascination' and 'thrill' and 'want'. I want that type of want. I nose my car into the gap behind stall number forty-four. My stall. I'm on the city side of the Laskin Beach boardwalk, so I score a parking spot.

Coming out to my parents is not an option. Much too terrifying. Not only am I disappointing them by not using my degree properly, I am—quote—dabbling in frivolity because the arts are a waste of time and simply a money pit—unquote. I can only imagine what adding 'lesbian' to that bottomless pit of disappointment will do. Knowing my mother, she'll state categorically that I can't be a lesbian because I've never had a girlfriend and therefore how on earth can I possibly have that much self-awareness? I know I am the biggest coward in the world. Look at yesterday's manager and the customer. Right there in the centre of the shopping mall. Declaring themselves with their smiles.

I give my driver's door a bit of a shove. Twenty-three years of age is a hell of a time to decide to choose art as a career, and gallivant about offering free legal advice to anyone who might need it. I'll have to coordinate the moment when I inform my parents about my new path in life with the arrival of the removal van.

I lug the two floor and three table-top easels into my sun shelter, lay them on the concrete, and hustle back for my folios. I have more prints with me today. The A4 high-quality reproductions of my paintings have sold well this week, so I figure that today will follow suit. At least I hope so. I set all my displays, making sure that the originals are draped in plastic—the salty film that settles on everything by the end of the day is unbelievably damaging, hence plastic, then I rack my prints, and hang my gorgeous banner that I made at OfficeMax. *Alexandria Sandonis Art*. I still get a buzz.

"Hey! Alexandria Sandonis is in the house!" yells a cheeky voice. I whip my head around, long brown ponytail swinging, and grin across the empty boardwalk to the stalls on the other side—basically four metres away. Zed—yes, like the last letter of the alphabet—leans her slim frame casually against her table, the digital camera loose in her hand, and the strap wrapped around her wrist. She's dressed in another version of the exact same outfit as the previous ten days that the market's been operating; tank top, cargo shorts, and sandals. Her sunglasses are perched in the nest of her messy short blonde hair, and I catch the glint of the two silver chains that drape about her neck. Zed is in her mid-thirties. I think. It's hard to tell. She's mischievous and irreverent and remarkably flirty. The skin near her blue eyes crinkles when she smiles. The lines of muscle and tendons in her forearms hold my attention whenever she wanders over to chat. Her greeting makes my stomach swoop and swirl in happiness. I have a ten-day-old crush.

"Morning, Zed. You going to have a good day?" I call back, then pluck at my shirt and flap it away from my body, cooling the sweat prickles. She watches.

"Absolutely. You too, hey? Want a hand with your tinsel?" She laughs as I glare at her. Yesterday I'd had the genius idea of hanging tinsel from the top of my shade tent. I'm a five feet three petite sprite. How on earth was I going to get three metres of tinsel hung that high up in the air, even with assistance? Anyway, it didn't happen, but it did create hilarity for Zed, Soma, and a number of other stall holders.

"Sorry. Christmas joy and cheer is cancelled at this stall today." I plant my hands on my hips to underline the statement.

Zed tilts her laptop, adjusts her card payment device, and shifts her weight to the other foot, all without breaking eye contact. "That's a shame, Alex. I really like your joy and cheer." Then she lifts a corner of her mouth in a little smile and winks. I blush.

After a quick check on my stall, and an even quicker check on my customer-service face in my phone camera—bright brown eyes, a touch of make-up that hopefully won't slide off in the midday heat—I'm ready for another market day on Laskin Beach boardwalk.

And what a great day it is! The locals are relaxed. The tourists are excited and hilarious. Those that stop to browse make the time for small talk, which is nice. At lunchtime, I meet Linda and Grant, in their matching golf shirts and shorts, as they stop at my stall. They tell me that they're from New York and express their astonishment at how vibrant Melbourne is; the strangeness of having Christmas in summer and their general bemusement at road rules, accent, and vocabulary. My laughter joins theirs. They buy one of my originals, which is incredible so I thrust out the card machine that I've leased for the duration of the market and they send one thousand dollars zipping into my account. It's breathtaking. I am selling my art and the idea that I could do this for a living settles happily in my heart.

The piece that Linda and Grant have bought is of the old wooden rollercoaster—the kind without loops but with twists and turns and clinks and clanks—inside the fun park at the end of the beach. Even now, the screams from the people in the old-fashioned two-seater carriages as they complete their climb and fall over the rise into the first curve drift in the breeze to compete with the bossy screeching of the seagulls who undulate in the air over people's lunches. To catch sight of the ride's white wooden framing, I have to look across the boardwalk and past the far stalls. Zed's stall, particularly. She uses the rollercoaster as the backdrop for her photographs. The sky today is a cerulean blue, and with the stark white wooden slats supporting the silver track, I imagine her portraits will be even more stunning.

I've seen the thumbnails she sends to the customers immediately after their photo is taken. She's very talented. Nearly every person, especially the couples, buy the full-size print, watch it land in their Dropbox or wherever and then complete the transaction. I lower my gaze and, in between the gaps of people in the crowd flowing past, I watch her. She's focused and unaware of my observation. Until she's not. Her gaze catches mine and my reward is another cheeky grin and a wave. Talk about rollercoaster twists and turns.

I start to break down my stall at six o'clock. The customers have wandered off home or to a nearby restaurant, and even though the market operates until eight because of daylight saving, the soft, muted light of the evening is too dim to showcase my work. It's fine, though. It's been another fun day.

"What is all this, Alexandria?"

The furiously hissed whisper is a dart into my neck, and I spin to find my mother vibrating with a range of emotions in the dark of my tent.

"God, Mum. What are you doing here?" I step away from my table and meet her in the middle of my space. My safe, secure space. She's obviously slipped in through the flap in the back panel.

"What am I doing here? I should be asking you the same question," she seethes. Then she sweeps her arm in the direction of my work, of my table, of my happiness. "How dare you embarrass our family name by commandeering a...by participating in this market! I knew you were becoming overly involved in your painting but this is beyond the pale." She grasps my shoulders. "Thank goodness Janice told me about...this when her daughter told her that she'd seen your sign. This is beneath you."

My trembling body is probably the only reason I can shake out of her grip. "No, it's not, Mum. I love my art, and I'm good at it. Even today, I sold one of my paintings for the sticker price." I swallow. "I got a thousand for it." Dollar amounts are a feature of Mum's vocabulary, so dropping that little gem might help this appalling situation.

"Then put your paintings in a gallery, for heaven's sake. Then they'll be sold properly and you can concentrate on your career."

"This is—" With a deep breath inside my lungs, and courage from God knows where, I say it. "This is my career, Mum. I want to paint, and teach painting, and meet customers and talk about my work, and give my time to the asylum seekers centre." I toss my hands in frustration. "I'm going to do this, whether you respect it or not." Holy crap.

Her gasp is a sort of cough, sort of huff, sort of rough screech. I've hit the limit of her disappointment meter.

"Your step-father and I haven't put good money into your education for you to throw it away on painting pretty pictures and supplying free legal services for those who have jumped the queue."

Rage.

"Oh my God, Mum. It is not illegal to seek asylum in another country and there is no queue. I can't believe I have to keep repeating myself."

She leans in. "You have a trust fund, young lady. Fix up the shambles of your career, apply yourself properly for the sake of our name, and your step-father's re-election, and you can access it when you're thirty." Her voice is rising. "Otherwise, nothing, do you hear? We will not be granting access to it for…this carry on."

I want to cry. The wobble in my voice sounds weak, so I give it some grit.

"I don't care about the trust fund, Mum. I want to follow my dream and…" I lose my nerve.

"We'll talk about this situation at home tonight," Mum says, as if she hasn't come all the way down to the beach to talk about the situation now. She delivers an irritated head shake, like she's annoyed by the summer flies, and swishes out through the flap. I feel sick.

"You okay, Alex?"

It's Zed, carefully collecting my prints, layering them together, and gazing at my face in concern.

I walk over and press my hands onto the table top. "I'm…oh God, Zed. What am I going to do?"

She hums. "I don't exactly know what the problem is, but I do know the solution." She continues to pack my art, then I notice that her stall is empty, and she's placed her roller suitcase containing her laptop, prints, and cameras next to the side panel of my shelter.

"What's the solution?" I ask, folding up the easels.

"Alcohol and food, preferably laden with carbs, salt, and cheese."

I pause, squint at her blue-eyed innocent expression, and laugh. It feels good. Then panic strikes. What if I'm late home for the follow up 'chat'? Come on, I'm twenty-three, for heaven's sake.

"You know? You're right. Where do we find this solution?"

"I might know somewhere," she says. We nod in time, grinning, and something in me glows, like a string of Christmas lights when all the bulbs have been replaced.

Zed suggests the *Lion's Head*, a pub on the side road up the city end of Wilkins Street. Then she tells me that her minuscule flat is around the corner from the pub, so having bundled my work, Zed's suitcase, and Zed into my car, I park it outside her place in the designated spot.

We walk around the corner, and angle past the A-frame chalkboard in the doorway advertising their Christmas dinner of chicken parma and chips. A corner table beckons, and we slide in so that we're sitting opposite each other. I lift my elbows like a baby bird and bathe in the air-conditioning, as Zed taps a message into her phone, then flips it over onto the table.

"A couple of friends are meeting me tonight, and I was just letting them know I'm already here," she says.

"Oh! I'm sorry. I'm crashing your catch-up."

Zed reaches across the table and folds her slim fingers over my hand. "No. You're not. I'm meeting friends, and you're a friend." She smiles crookedly, and I'm aware of her touch. Actually, I'm aware of a lot because her nearness over-stimulates my body. The conversations, the cricket playing on the TV that's hung on the wall at the far end, the soft instrumental carols playing through hidden speakers. Hyper-aware.

I clear my throat, and slide my hand back. "Well, thank you. You've saved me from going home immediately. My procrastination attempts for the foreseeable future will be epic as I avoid the next confrontation with my mum."

"Was that what was going on before?"

"Oh yeah. Okay. Quick summary is that I have a law degree, which I use to do pro bono work at the main asylum seekers centre in," I waggle my finger in the general direction of the Melbourne city centre, and she nods, "and I paint, which you know. And I'd been gearing myself up to finally tell my mum and step-dad that I need to move out, that I want to pursue art as my career and that I want to continue to do the pro bono work, but I guess it all came out today." I wince slightly at the 'coming out' line. The other coming out is a long way off.

"Ah," Zed says, nodding in sympathy. "Yeah, that's…"

"Yep." I run my fingernail into a groove in the wood. "The upshot is that I'm a massive disappointment, that I should know better, and that I'm embarrassing my family name."

I receive a deep exhale as my response, and look up. Zed pulls her lips sideways in thought.

"I know who your family is, Alex. I can't help knowing, actually, because your step-dad's campaign is pretty conservative. I pay attention to conservative politics because it generally impacts on my not-at-all-conservative life." She grins, and shrugs. "We're more than our family name, Alex. Think of Sandonis as the brand of camera." She flicks her finger at me. "You're the lens. You get to change the perspective and how far you want to view the world." We hold each other's gaze, then I smile.

"I like that."

Zed laughs. "It's not a great analogy, but I work with what I've got."

"I like what you've got," I blurt out, and instantly my eyes widen and I am absolutely positive my breath freezes in my chest. Oh crap. Luckily, Zed simply raises an eyebrow, spreads out the cardboard coasters across the table, and asks me what I'd like to drink. I mutter something, possibly house wine, and force the blush from my face. By the time she's back with my wine—well done, me—and her bourbon, I've pulled myself together and deflect the topic of conversation back to her.

"My drama probably seems silly. You're so put together." I sip from my glass, happily acknowledging the fact that I'd rather be drinking a cheap, rough red in a pub in suburban seaside Melbourne with a kind, sympathetic, very hot woman, than an expensive, pretentious merlot in a mansion with my step-dad's sycophants.

"I am now. I wasn't for a while." She runs a thumb over her bottom lip. "I'm a lesbian, if you weren't aware." Zed winks, and I shift subtly on my seat, thrilled at the little shiver. "Anyway, for a long time I was incredibly concerned about what other people in my life thought of me. I was unhappy, and it occurred to me that if I changed that thinking and based my happiness on facts rather than the belief of others, then I'd be much more comfortable. So, now I fact check. Am I happy with who I am? Yes. Did it make me happy to help you out today? Yes. Does it make me happy having a drink with you in a pub on Christmas Eve's Eve's Eve? Yes."

I giggle into my wine at her silliness. Zed's eyes sparkle, then she stares intently at me. "No one should be afraid of who they are, Alex." She's not talking about my career choice. She knows, and there's a moment.

"I think I'm a lesbian, too," I whisper across the table, and I swallow. Then, as Zed holds my hand, everything pours out. "Oh, God! I can't believe I just said that. I mean, in this day and age and in this city, I should be able to easily come out as anything I like. God, at Uni, everyone around me was flinging open closet doors. They were all rainbow unicorns and I was this closeted straight-acting freak with seriously restrictive parents who monitored my friendships. And even though they're my parents and I do love them, if I come out as a lesbian, they'll do something crazy like bundle me into conversion therapy because you saw what—"

"Alex."

"—Mum was like this afternoon, and that was just about deciding on a choice of career. Imagine what she'd be—"

"Alex!"

I jerk my head, instantly cutting off the blathering.

Zed squeezes my hand. "Firstly, you can come out any old time you like. Secondly, yeah, I figured you might be." Another hand squeeze. "And lastly, would you really be sent to therapy?" That earns me a look of concern.

"No. But the repercussions…I just can't."

"Okay."

"But I want to."

"Okay."

"I really want to. I really do." The intent in my stare can't be stronger.

Zed chews her lip. "Then do it." She leans closer, so I smell the sunscreen on her skin, like a permanent summer perfume. "Open the door, Alex. The world is waiting."

"Are you?" I blink. "I mean, is it?"

"Absolutely. Now," she shuffles in her seat, "practice on me."

"What?"

"Let's role play. I'll be your parents." She frowns and purses her lips. "Alexandria, darling, you said you had something to tell us." Her voice is theatrical, and I dissolve into a fit of giggles, which is the state her friends find us in when they arrive not a minute later.

Zed whips through the introductions—Gee, short for Geena, maybe about late-twenties, is a receptionist at a real estate agency and has clearly come straight from work based on her outfit, and her girlfriend, Liv, short for Olivia, mid-thirties, is a graphic designer and is obviously allowed to wear whatever she likes because she's dressed in cargo shorts, and a tank top, like Zed. They grab their drinks and settle in around the table; Gee next to Zed, and Liv beside me.

"So, what's happening?" Liv ping-pongs her gaze between Zed and me.

"Alex is coming out."

I splutter-cough into my wine. "Oh my God," I gasp, glaring at Zed, who laughs.

"We're role-playing it now. I'm her parents."

Gee claps once. "Terrific. Liv and I'll be the judgemental relatives."

I find my voice. "We can't do this here!"

Zed leans her chin on her palm. It's kind of sexy. "Sure we can. This is probably just as uncomfortable as doing it at home. Think of it as a rehearsal."

"Oh my God," I say again. "This is insane. Okay." I shake my head. "Okay." I stare hard at Zed, and both of us are doing our best not to laugh. "Mum. I have something to tell you."

Zed's lips quirk. "Is it about that young man from Uni?"

Gee jumps in. "I've heard good things about him. Upstanding citizen, that one."

"Comes from good stock." Liv's contribution sends us into gales of laughter, and I drink more wine.

"This is not going to work," I say through more laughter.

"Yes, it is. Try it," Zed says earnestly. "Come on."

My breath is deep. "Here we go." I gaze at Zed. "I'm a lesbian and I want to live my truth and I know it's Christmas and to you, that means everything has to be perfect because apparently Christmas is about the right presentation and the best wrapping and having the nicest cutlery and not making waves." I inhale. "But I'm still your daughter who also happens to be a lesbian, and that's my perfect, which means I don't have any wrapping paper left to hide inside. Here I am. I'm me."

Tears fill my eyes, and a number of things happen at once. Zed grabs my hands in one of her own, softly wipes my tears with the thumb of her other hand, and smiles into my face. Gee leaps from her seat and hustles to the bar with the plastic-coated menu, and Liv pats my back, then inexplicably pulls a black Sharpie from her pocket, and starts gathering in the dry coasters.

"You're brave, Alex," Zed whispers, as Liv's arm shoots across the table, flicking the cardboard squares towards herself.

I'm still holding onto her hands. "I'm not really."

"No, you're not, then."

That's surprising. "Oh?"

"No. Bravery is just courage that forgot its crash helmet." She bends her elbows to bring me closer, our eyes fixed on each other's faces. "So, you're courageous."

Gee lands with a thump and distributes baskets of chips and little pots of tomato sauce and mayonnaise about the table.

"Dig in. I've got other nibbles coming later." She points to me. "Good job with the coming out, by the way. It was like you'd had that speech stored up for a while." She smiles knowingly and I want to hug her. Instead, I dunk a chip into the mayonnaise and bite off the end.

"All right. Next round's on me. First up, though," Liv pauses dramatically and individually grabs our attention. "Never have I ever."

Zed groans. "I am nowhere near drunk enough for that, Liv."

"You will be." She brandishes the Sharpie, yanks the lid off, and writes 'I have' and 'I have not' on either side of four coasters, and passes one to each of us. I flip mine around like a little affirmative negative fan, and wait for the catch. Liv enlightens us.

"Okay. What are we drinking at? Have or have not?" She leans sideways to look at me. "Alex, you pick."

"Um. All right. Have not," I say, and instantly I recognise my potential for outright drunkenness. My life experience is not vast. Oh dear.

It soon becomes apparent that Liv, Gee and Zed have no interest in drinking on their negative. Their affirmative answers also qualify. But no one is on their way to becoming shit-faced, or even tipsy for that matter. I feel warm, from being with people who understand me, from the bit of wine, from the appreciative heated looks I'm receiving from Zed.

"Okay, shush, you lot. My turn," I say, and smile inwardly at my sass, enjoying how it sounds from my mouth. "Never have I ever… gone to the toilet too many times to avoid awkward moments at a Christmas dinner." Gee smacks the table-top in laughter, as the others hold up their coasters. I point to each as I say their answers aloud. "You have and you have," I laugh at Zed and Liv. Gee shakes her head and flashes her 'I have not' at me.

All three heads turn in my direction, and I pause for dramatic effect. "Christmas three years ago, my mum rang the doctor because she was worried I had gastroenteritis as I'd spent more time in the toilet than at the table."

Zed throws her hands into the air, and shouts, "Winner!" Liv and Gee applaud my effort, Zed's blue eyes connect with mine and I want to kiss her.

"My turn," Zed insists. "Never have I ever…worn handcuffs." She grins wickedly at Gee, who narrows her eyes and points.

"It was one time, you bastard, and I can't believe I told you—" She doesn't get to finish because she is swept up in Liv's one-arm hug and our laughter.

"Oh, sweetheart. Anyone can lose the keys. Really," Liv says, and I hold my coaster to my chest, the 'I have not' facing out because… handcuffs.

Drinks and more dinner bits arrive at various points in the evening, and then all too soon, I'm hugging Liv and Gee goodbye and I'm walking around the corner with Zed. She grabs her stuff from my car and we stop at the red front door to her ground floor flat.

"Thank you for everything, Zed. Today and tonight," I say, my hands clasping together then sliding into the pockets of my shorts, then out again. Zed stills their movements with her own hands.

"You're welcome. As I said, I think you're courageous and I've enjoyed getting to know you even more tonight. You're a lot of fun, Alex." Her eyes are searching, and I look up and over her shoulder, taking in the little plastic mistletoe wreath hanging above the door. I decide to be courageous again.

"Zed?" I whisper. "Did you know that the largest mistletoe in the world grows in Australia?"

"No, I didn't."

"Zed?" I focus on her lips, then her eyes, which are bright.

"Yeah?" She brings my hands together against her shirt.

"Never have I ever kissed someone under mistletoe," I say, and I feel the enormous breath she takes. "I know you're interested," I add quietly.

"I am, Alex, but I'd never—"

"What if I want you to?" I step a tiny bit closer and look up into her face.

"Alex, you're gorgeous and oh wow, you're sexy as…but you only came out tonight. I can't—"

"But I can," I breathe. "It's sex, if we happen to get there, with no strings, no wrapping paper. I'm an adult, Zed, and I know what this means." She stares at me for ages, then releases my hands to cup my face. She leans closer and softly brushes her lips against mine. My eyes close, I sink in, and it feels automatic to hold the sides of her head with my hands. When she withdraws, I wait for the next kiss. But then I don't and push up on my toes to press hot lips against her mouth. She's so soft.

Zed pulls away, rummages in her pocket for her keys, quickly opens the door, and bundles the suitcase inside. Then she's standing in the doorway, holding my hands, waiting.

"God, Alex. Are you sure? I'm clean, and tested. Whatever you say goes, absolutely, because we can just talk and kiss if you want, and—"

I kiss her again, my lips sliding between hers. Her mouth is salty from the sea air, and sweet from the bourbon. "Yes, I'm very sure. And all that other stuff is important and necessary and sounds wonderful, but can we say it to each other inside where it's cooler?"

She looks at me like I'm the best present she's ever received. I'm pretty sure my expression is a mirror image. "Okay." Her smile is filled with wonder.

"Okay," I whisper. "You know? This is the first Christmas I get to be me."

Zed slides her hands down, cups my bum, and lifts me so that I can wrap my legs around her waist. She peppers my lips and cheeks with quick kisses, walking us into her flat, then holds me while she closes and locks the door. "Then let's make it a very happy Christmas."

Finding Faith

I really need to ride to work more often. Catching public transport is great, but it's a kick in the guts when I have to cycle the ten kilometres. I mean, it takes me about half an hour, and then I'm a panting, sweaty mess at the end. Just as well work has showers. But taking the bike is necessary today. Of all the days for the tram drivers to go on strike, two days before Christmas is not ideal. I guess it's ideal for them, because they're making a point about pay and stuff and inconveniencing passengers makes their point more obvious. Anyway, good on them. So, I'm biking it.

I whip across the extra lane of traffic and duck into Wilkins Street. Normally, I'd stop at the *BargainBuy* and grab my lunch for the day, but I made it at home this morning. Good job, me. Lunch is shoved in between the pieces of the dark-blue uniform and underwear in my backpack. Thank all the heavens that I don't have to trundle my boots back and forth. My locker keeps those safe and sound.

The boardwalk is narrow as I get closer to Laskin Beach, so I slow down, and eventually get off and walk my bike through the market. I've got time. My shift doesn't start for another forty-five minutes and the branch is only a kilometre away, down the end of Beach Road which runs along the foreshore. Sapphy will already be there, checking the truck for all the meds and gear. She's straight down the line, that one, which is good because she's the qualified paramedic. Pays to be pedantic. That'll be me in a year.

I pause in my thoughts when I see Nyaring, her backpack draped over one shoulder, talking to one of the stallholders halfway along the boardwalk. It looks like she's already been for a run this morning; the speckles of wet sand on her strong legs shine like glitter on her dark skin. Everything about her shines so brightly. She's wonderful. Nyaring is a friend and a lifeguard on Laskin Beach, and because she's already decked out in her red shorts and long-sleeved yellow shirt with 'SURF RESCUE' emblazoned across the back, then I reckon I know where she's heading. We've known each other for about six months, initially because we kept crossing paths, being in similar lines of work. Usually, I'd turn up with Sapphy because someone at the patrol tower rang for an ambulance. If it was the weekend, Nyaring would be one of the team on patrol. We'd talk. But two weeks ago, she started doing more shifts, then this week leading up to Christmas, she's been here every day. Her boss at her job as a dental hygienist gives her the time off, which is very cool. She reckons that working in her own community, the South Sudanese community, means that she can explain why volunteering is important and so she gets the time off to do it. I like that. I like being her friend. Nyaring wears a stillness. There's a sense of containment and place, and I want to just sit next to her and be.

I slide to a stop, and grin. Her tightly-cropped hair, a halo about her head, is also slightly speckled with sand.

"Hey Nyaring. How're ya doing?"

She does that lovely thing with her face, where her mouth only moves a little bit to create a smile, but her velvet midnight skin relaxes, her eyes twinkle, and she looks at me like I'm important. I'd pretty much do anything for her. And it's not about lust, infatuation, a crush, or anything like that. It's more a case of seeing each other. She said that to me in not so many words only a month ago.

"You're a very good person, Kate. You do more than accept people, you embrace them, and I think that is a wonderful quality." I could have floated home on those words.

"I'm well, Kate. How are you?"

"Awesome. Sweaty." I rotate my shoulders to move the backpack straps about.

She laughs quietly, then gestures with her hand towards the petite woman behind the table. "Kate, this is Alex. We have been discussing some of the work at the Asylum Seekers Centre. Alex volunteers her legal expertise."

"Cool!" I say, nodding in appreciation, then I point to her banner in front of me. "I haven't seen you at the markets before. Your art is really good."

Alex's eyes light up. "Thank you! I've only joined this Christmas and it's been so fantastic." Her enthusiasm is adorable. "Do you work nearby?"

I lean my bike against my hip. "Yeah. I'm an ambo down at the Beach Road branch." I wave my whole hand at Nyaring, knowing she's uncomfortable with a one-finger point. "That's how I know Nyaring. We have similar clientele, although hers are more soggy."

Alex laughs, and Nyaring presses her lips together like I'm an amusing, but harmless, puppy. You'd never know we were the same age.

I grin. "So what's the latest at the Centre?"

Alex answers. "We're looking for another South Sudanese translator because we can't ask the other Arabic speakers."

"Why n—?" I cut myself off because I remember Nyaring explaining that Sudanese Arabic is a bit different. I nod. "Like Canadian French," I say, "and French…French."

"Exactly," they both say.

The whole time we've been chatting, Alex's attention has occasionally slid across to the other side of the boardwalk. To one stand in particular. The woman, in the final stages of setting up her photography stall, is also sending a lot of glances and some very heated looks in return. I catch Alex's blush. Oh, hello. There's something special going on here. I smile inwardly. I love stuff like this. The new. The freshness. The finding.

"You working Christmas Day, Nyaring?"

"Oh no. My family commitments override that. Besides Christmas Day is…" she fades off and I finish for her.

"A circus."

She nods in agreement, then adjusts her backpack. "Well, I need to get to work."

I swing my leg over my bike, and straddle the bar to hold it upright. "Yeah, me, too. Hope it's a quiet one for you." I look at Alex. "Although, not quiet for you. Sell heaps." We grin, Nyaring smiles, and I wave to her, as I duck-walk the bike between two stalls, jump on when I get to open space, and cycle down Beach Road.

Sapphy, as I thought, has sorted everything by the time I lock up my bike, fling my lunch into the communal fridge, shower, change into my uniform and shove my feet into my sturdy boots.

"Hey, Sapph." Not content with shortening her name from Sapphire to Sapphy, I tend to go one step further with 'Sapph'. It's an Australian thing, I reckon. A service station is a servo, a Christmas present is a Chrissy pressie. Anyway, Sapphy pokes her head out of the back doors, her neat blonde bun accessorising her crisp uniform.

"Hey there, yourself. You good?"

I climb into the passenger seat, toss my muesli bar into the cupholder, and turn into the middle so I can continue talking to her as she finishes up.

"Yeah. Bit tired, but. I stayed up half the night doing an assignment and everyone wouldn't shut up. It was hard yakka." Sapphy knows I live in a share house with four other people, in ages ranging from nineteen through to me at twenty-seven. It is noisy pretty much all the time. But I need to get this subject finished if I want to graduate at the end of September next year. Sometimes doing summer school is a blessing and a curse.

"But you got it done, right?" I hear the twin doors thump, and then she's leaning on the driver's seat through the open door.

"Yep. Submitted and everything." I cast my eye over the interior of the truck. Just a habit. Making sure nothing's out of place. A white pom-pom pokes out from under the floor mat. I reach down and pull free a cloth Santa hat, red with a white band and the pom-pom at the top. I give it a shake.

"Where'd this come from?"

Sapphy tosses a cursory glance, and focuses on her clipboard. "Dunno."

I smile. "Cool. I'll stick it on if we get a paeds call."

"You can't wear it when you're attending, Kate, even for kids."

"I know. I'll shove it away when I have to."

I'm driving for our first call an hour later because Sapphy is the attending, but it's an address only three streets away. Our patient is Frank, a frequent flyer. He's sixty and rings for an ambulance every twelve or thirteen days, usually for heart pain, which ends up being indigestion through to numbness in his feet, meaning he's sat in his armchair too long. Poor bugger is just lonely.

"Kate, how're ya, luv?" He groans from his armchair. Hmm. It's another bout of numbness. We run through the familiar routine, eventually get him settled onto the gurney in his driveway, and head towards the back of the truck. Sapphy whacks the doors open, as I hold Frank steady, so he doesn't go for an impromptu swim in the ocean three streets away.

"Oh dear, Frank!" A voice, pitched higher with concern, breaks into my thoughts. The slim woman, maybe older than Frank by a decade, stands on the footpath, clutching her green *BargainBuy* shopping bag. She flicks a worried gaze between me and our patient on the mobile stretcher.

"Don't worry, Nola. Got my girls looking after me, right? This is Kate." Frank, tips his head, and suddenly animated, flaps a hand towards the doors where Sapphy has appeared to guide the gurney inside. "That's Sapphy. She's a looker, yeah?"

Sapphy's eyes widen in annoyance, and she lifts her chin in a 'come on' gesture. I duly 'come on' and we get Frank sorted, Sapphy in the back, and me driving.

The triage nurse at Emergency looks at Frank's name on the chart and her thought bubble says, *Really?* She takes him off our hands and we head back to the branch. I bet Sapphy a chocolate bar that we'll see Frank again in eleven days, not twelve.

This time I'm in charge of vehicle restock, which is fair. The Santa hat is still in my pocket, and I don't get to wear it for the next two call outs, because they're strictly in and out. Into the residence, out to the hospital. Basic, non-life-threatening injuries. So I wear the hat in the lounge, munching on my now very late lunch with a cuppa, and collecting smiles from colleagues.

"Festive much?"

"O'course, Johnno. Gotta get in the spirit, mate." I even chuck in a *ho ho ho* at the end, which cracks him up.

Then, late in the afternoon, we get a lifeguard tower call out. A broken forearm, dislocated wrist, abrasions, all wrapped up in a very drunk bloke. Of course, that's not how Control spells it out, but I'm paraphrasing.

We park in the little concrete pad literally on the beach without being on the sand. It's been built specifically for ambulances and the quad bikes that the lifesavers use to tow the inflatable rescue boats into the shed. Gloves on, I grab the gear, Sapphy locks the truck, and immediately our boots sink into the yellowy white sand. Wearing black boots, dark blue cargo pants, dark blue short-sleeve shirt and carrying shit-loads of gear is not fun when the heat, shimmering off the sand, is eyeball-searing. Apparently, Christmas Day is going to be a scorcher. We get to the bottom of the tower, and find Nyaring, and Dave-o, one of the blue-shirted professional lifeguards, waiting with a sunburnt white guy, who's built like a small, squashed, rectangular prism. He's lying on one of their red moulded-plastic spinal boards. Nyaring, in the process of shrugging on her yellow shirt, nods at me, all business. She's been in the water, probably to rescue the drunk shirtless bloke at my feet. Sapphy and Dave-o, white zinc smeared across his nose and cheeks, are doing the handover, and I take in the important bits and pieces. Apparently, he's had a skinful and decided to go for a wander out on the rocks despite drinking all day, then he slipped and landed heavily on his idiot self, breaking his arm and dislocating his wrist. Again, paraphrasing.

"We gave him the green whistle only about ten minutes ago," Nyaring's soft, low voice floats from behind my head, as I bend down and check my patient, who's moaning and sucking on the lime-green Penthrox pain-relieving inhaler. He's wearing a pair of board shorts that are knee-length and sopping wet and I wonder again how blokes can wear them halfway down their bum with the material wrapping around their thighs so they end up waddling about like a drunk duck. Actually, that might explain today's situation.

"Hey mate, I'm Kate. I'm an ambulance officer. I need to know if you have any ID on you?"

Through tiny slits in his eyelids, he makes eye contact and mumbles around the mouthpiece of the whistle. I catch the words 'back pocket', so I feel quickly and sure enough there's a damp wallet, which I fish out and flip open, finding the driver's license at the front.

"Can you tell me your name, mate?"

"Paul." He inhales. "Harrison," he finishes.

I check. Right, he knows who he is. Always a good thing. I look up at Nyaring. "You pulled him out?"

"Not pulled him out, exactly. The rocks were above the water line, but the waves create large, shallow pools and when I saw him slip, I wanted to get there as soon as possible in case he had a head injury, and the way he landed meant that he might have drowned."

It's a succinct summary and downplays the fact that she's potentially saved his life. Sapphy and Dave-o, at either end of the plastic stretcher, deliver a soft countdown and then lift Paul the Completely Plastered—now looking much more comfortable and medically cared for—into the air and we trudge back through the soft sand to the truck. My door-opening-gurney-pulldown is well-practised, and in no time, we've transferred Paul, who's now giggling and as high as a kite from the Penthrox, onto the wheeled stretcher. Nyaring steps forward to retrieve the lightweight board.

"Ready, Paul? We'll get you to hospital, okay, mate?" He swings his head, his eyeballs following with a slight delay, and smiles dopily.

"Yeaahhh," he drawls, then waves the inhaler randomly. "Want some more of this stuff, but. Black chick gave me this one and it's nearly run out."

I jerk my head back, flicking my eyes from our patient who's staring at the blue sky and smiling, to Sapphy, who pauses ever so slightly before continuing on with her paperwork, to Nyaring, whose face has closed down. Dave-o has already wandered back down to the beach.

I return my gaze to Paul, and very carefully, very casually, say, "Paul, her name's Nyaring and she's a lifesaver."

He blinks at me, then lifts his head to stare blearily down the end of the gurney at my friend. "She can't be a lifesaver, mate. Refugees can't swim. We're always bloody pulling them out of the water when they're trying to get into the fucking country." He grunts as he drops his head, and I feel like I've been punched in the stomach. I stare at Nyaring. Her liquid brown eyes are filled with hurt. Then Sapphy calls my name. I want to comfort Nyaring, but I need to get moving. So I do the only thing that makes me feel like I'm helping. I lean over, and, summoning the flattest, broadest Australian accent I have, based on years of growing up in the country, I growl into his face.

"Listen, mate. You're fucking lying here 'cause you're a drunk dickhead with a busted arm. But you're also a racist dickhead, and you can count all your Christmas blessings, mate, 'cause if Nyaring wasn't so good at her job, you woulda drowned. Then you'd be a dead racist dickhead, so shut your stupid white mouth and we'll take you to see a doctor, okay?"

I'm shaking when I start the truck, and we drive the fifteen minutes through the city to the hospital. After handover, Sapphy and I sit quietly in the front of the truck for a moment.

"As your senior colleague, I don't recommend saying stuff like that to patients," Sapphy says, staring through the windscreen at the full ambulance parking bay outside the emergency department.

I nod slowly. "I couldn't let it slide, though, Sapph. What an arsehole."

"I know. I get that. But it's not our place to moralise. We're not meant to get involved in politics."

I spin in my seat, collecting the steering wheel with my elbow. "Ow. But it's not politics. It's right and wrong."

Her blue eyes meet mine. "I know. It sucks."

"I hate how alcohol and the heat and Christmas in general just brings out the fuckers."

Sapphy laughs softly. "Come on, Kate. Good Time Paul isn't a one-off. Maybe the Penthrox loosened his tongue, but the words were already there, ready to be set free by a magic green whistle or alcohol." She stares at me again, a tiny twitch in her lips. "I thought you were going to do your block, though."

I laugh. "Nah. I said what I said. Mind you, I coulda done a job on his other arm. Given him a matching pair."

Back at the branch, I realise my Santa hat, which has warmed my pocket all day, has disappeared, and I assume it's buried in the sand on Laskin Beach somewhere. Oh well. I change clothes, pack up my gear into my backpack, and stow my boots in my locker for tomorrow, which is bound to be full of dehydration call-outs, and more Pauls. Then I've got Christmas Day off and Boxing Day as well, which is a nice score. With a cheery bye to everyone, I wheel my bike out the staff door, around the corner, and literally run into Nyaring standing on the path that leads to the main office.

"Hey! How're you going?" I grin.

She shoulders her backpack, her red shorts now replaced with lightweight red and yellow track pants, and smiles with her whole face. She's holding the Santa hat.

"I'm okay now, Kate. Thank you. I wanted to return this. It dropped from your pocket when you were attending to the patient." I take the hat, smile my thanks, but don't speak because I can see she's not finished. "Also, I wanted to thank you for what you said to him. It was very noble. I hope that you didn't get into trouble."

I shake my head, and I tuck the hat into the outside pocket of my backpack. Then I flick my brown fringe out of my face.

"Nope. Sapph said something, which she kinda has to, and Paul's never gonna say anything. He won't remember the actual day, let alone what a cranky ambo said to him." I look her up and down. "You need to get going? Or do you want to grab a burger or something and eat on the rock wall?"

She tilts her head. Something else I admire. Nyaring's never flippant, so ideas are given proper consideration. "Yes. What about the fish and chip restaurant opposite the tower towards the markets? Would that do?"

"Absolutely! Love their food."

As we turn onto the main footpath, Sapphy appears between the trucks, then walks out onto the driveway to meet a pair of women;

one in a business outfit and heels, the other carrying camera gear. Looks like media. Sapphy is normally the one tapped on the shoulder to do interviews. The media likes very white. And very pretty. Even more so at Christmas, I've noticed. It's that cultural cringe phenomenon. Apparently, we don't like to see our country reflected back at us, so we fill our screens with white, American-accented, make-up-enhanced folk, who frolic through snow. And bake pies.

The seagulls dart about on the sand, squawking like they're still auditioning for *Finding Nemo*. I balance the parcel of wrapped-up chips on the wide bricks between us, tear a hole in the paper and we take turns to pull them out one at a time. Nyaring has bought a veggie burger, and I've gone for my usual—burger with salad, beetroot, egg, pineapple. One of the other ambos reckons that no other country in the world does a burger like that. Only Australia. I did a search on the Internet and it turns out it's true. The fish and chip place—calling it a restaurant is hyperbolic—lists it on their menu as an Aussie burger, so they must be right. Our legs dangle over the very low wall, skimming the sand banked up at the bottom.

I nudge my bike so it leans properly against the wall, then bite into the bread clutched in my fingers, and swallow.

"Did the rest of your day go okay?" I shield my eyes from the setting sun, and turn my face in her direction.

"Yes." She's chewing carefully. It makes me sad again.

"I hate stuff like that happening to you. To people. I dunno. It's like us white folk are jealous of cultures that are so centred, so contained and layered, so old and laden with passion, that we're filled with hate and want to bring those cultures down and shatter them, so that they are just as messed up as our fractured pile." My bite is enormous, and I chew for ages. After a while, I hear a single hum.

"That is an interesting perspective."

It's a kind of non-committal answer and I worry I've offended her. "Um…sorry?" There are apologetic wrinkles in my forehead.

"What for?" She gives me another head tilt.

"In case what I said just then was rude, or something."

Nyaring studies me. I wonder what she sees. Does she see a solidly-built woman with mousy brown hair and no real discernible features?

"Please stop walking on eggshells, Kate. If I was ever offended by something you might say," she lifts an elegant hand at me, "which I can guarantee won't happen, knowing you, then I would let you know. I think people get caught up worrying that they may offend someone accidentally, but unless a person is deliberately setting out to be offensive, then most errors are from a place of genuine ignorance, and can be easily rectified." She plucks a piece of tomato from inside her burger and pops it into her mouth. After a second, she swallows. "I've been aware ever since the first day we met that you don't swear around me, except, of course, for that very inventive collection today for Paul's benefit." Her smile is brilliant and there's that humour. I crack up.

"Yeah, well, that was a special occasion. I mean, I do swear. A lot. But I noticed that day we met—the older woman who'd fainted near the tower?" I receive a nod in acknowledgement. "Yeah, that day. Dave-o was having a yack with the other blokes and swearing away and you looked really uncomfortable. I wasn't sure if it was because they were being blokes, but I figured you have three brothers, so it couldn't be that, so I went with the swearing thing."

She beams at me. "See? Astute, and deliberately trying to not offend. It's respectful."

I stare out at the water. The ocean is quiet at dusk in Melbourne. It's a strange quirk. The waves'll pick up again once it's dark.

"Hey." I turn to her. "How are you getting home? We can pack up and go if you want to be on public transport before dark." Tension shimmers in my body.

She does that slow palm-lift again. "No. I'll text Achol later. He or Okot can pick me up in my father's car."

"They won't mind?"

"I highly doubt it. My parents," she pauses, "would chuck a pink fit if the boys ever grumble about doing a favour for another member of the family." The common idiom sounds so unfamiliar in Nyaring's cultured voice, and it makes me chuckle. She smiles again, and bites into her burger.

I restrain myself from tossing a chip at the seagulls. It's the next beach rule you learn after using sunscreen, drinking water, and swimming between the red and yellow flags. Don't feed the seagulls. The crazy scene in that bird horror movie from last century is exactly what happens.

"So asking questions is good, right?"

"Of course."

"Good, 'cause I've got a couple if that's okay, and I know it means you're doing the heavy lifting, so to speak, but it's hard when someone just tells you to nick off and google it."

"I promise not to tell you to nick off, Kate." Her statement is chased by that composed laugh, the one which is low and tells me that I'm safe to keep talking.

"So, you're the oldest at twenty-seven." I point to myself. "Same as me. Then Achol is twenty?" I lift the end of the word, and she nods. "And Okot is eighteen, which I know because you told me last month that he wanted to hire some warehouse for his party and the very thought of babysitting a billion newly-hatched adults made your teeth ache."

Our shared laughter is loud.

"And Abdo is in Year Ten, so…fifteen?"

"Yes. And focussed completely on soccer. My father is going to request that Abdo's teachers write his curriculum on the individual leather hexagons on the soccer balls because it will be the only way he pays attention."

I snort. We chew our food, and watch the slowing down of the day. The colours in the sky start to resemble that burnt filter on Instagram.

"I know that you work as an ambulance officer, and that you're studying to become a paramedic, but have you always lived here in Melbourne?" Her question is tentative.

I roll my shoulders, and sigh. Nyaring's eyes widen. "Oh! I'm sorry. Now I've offended you."

I mirror her soft palm-lift. "No, you haven't. I'm just mentally chucking the dates in order." I slide out a chip, bite the end off, and push the remainder in straight after, so my mouth is full of fried potato and I've got time to think.

"I'm from country Victoria. A little town called Neilson. You'd think there was a speck of dirt on your phone screen if you were looking for it on Google Maps. It's that tiny. Anyway, my parents are really religious. Church is a big deal in Neilson." I laugh without humour. "Religion and churches don't mean the same thing. Anyway, I'm getting ahead of myself. I wasn't great at school. I did okay, but I had opinions, no working filter, and things to sort out about myself that made other people uncomfortable. So, at eighteen I finished school and bummed around at jobs in town, like at the petrol station, volunteered for my church, then at twenty-four I decided to get my diploma to be an ambo." Another large bite of food disappears into my mouth. Nyaring glances at me, then continues to gaze at the sinking sun. "So, I had to drive two hours each way to Tohins to go to the community college there, but I did the twelve-month diploma and passed everything first time. Kinda proud of myself for that."

Nyaring smiles. "Absolutely."

My smile fades. "Yeah, but, you know how I said I had lots of opinions, no filter, and things to sort out?"

She nods carefully, her dark eyes intent.

"Well, turns out telling my parents and my church that I'm a lesbian wasn't a smart move, and I was promptly kicked out of home and the church and my town."

She breathes out heavily, like I've punched her with my story. "Oh, Kate. That's awful."

"Yeah. Yeah it is." My hand drifts towards the chip packet, and I pinch a small piece which is mostly crunchy batter, but I decide that I'm not hungry. "Anyway, there I was with a fresh qualification, a beaten-up car, and a suitcase. So, I came here." The little piece of chip rises at the word, and the seagulls lift off the sand in anticipation, hover, then land in disappointment. "Hey. That was yesterday! Two years ago, yesterday. Happy anniversary to a new life." I wave the chip towards her, and her smile is happy and sad and understanding and she picks up her own chip and we tap them together.

"For me, also. Today is the fifteen-year anniversary that my family achieved Australian citizenship. I was twelve."

"Oh, that's so cool. Hang on…" I quickly do the calculations, and gasp. "You came here when you were five. It took seven years to get citizenship? That's ridiculous!" Anger at injustices, bureaucratic and otherwise, bubbles inside.

"Of course." Her acceptance of that appalling fact is awful and I feel impotent, because I don't know how to fix the system. Then she continues. "We have a lot in common, Kate."

"Sure," I say sceptically.

"We do. We've both received life-changing Christmas presents which we appreciate and celebrate each year. We are refugees with our own stories."

I pull my head back. "Nope. No way. There's no way my story about being turfed out of home is anything like your story. Far out, Nyaring, you lived through war the first four and half years of your life, then you lived here in Melbourne probably on one of those humanitarian visas, which meant that you were unable to access services." She nods. "And because of that, I know that life has been really, really hard."

"Yes. It has. But our experiences are not in competition, Kate. You're here, right now, because your place of birth is no longer a place to live."

I'm blinking a lot.

"I still haven't found my place yet," I mumble, and instantly hope the sounds of the market, and the tinny music from the fish and chip shop whisk away my sentence.

Of course, she hears it. "I'm sorry that you haven't found that sense of culture or heritage. That deep place inside." Then she looks horrified, her eyes wide. "Oh. That's…Kate, again I'm making assumptions."

I laugh. "Oh gosh, look at us. Okay," I say, turning my head. "We're friends having an after-work chat and we're discovering interesting stuff about each other and we might put our foot in it, but it's okay. Deal?"

She grins, white teeth flashing, and eats a chip. "Deal."

"So, back to your comment. You're right. My sense of place is messy and it's a work in progress. I've got my Christian faith which I've cobbled back together again since living in Melbourne, but my heritage is...well, I'm a cooking pot of leftovers. So, I'm making my own places and filling my own spaces with the Philosophy of Kate."

Her smile is quick, and thoughtful.

A group of four teenage boys wanders past, filling their temporary space in life with choppy sentences, and gangly limbs, and bravado. They seem to prompt Nyaring's next question.

"Will you be spending Christmas with a girlfriend?"

"Nope. Don't have one." Then my brain decides to overshare. "I never really wanted to zip about having sex when I came to Melbourne. Still don't. I think I've wanted to find the bigger picture first. So many people are vibrating with tension all the time. They move like little atoms. I'm not made that way. I...want to pull the threads of Kate together first."

"I understand that." Her food long forgotten, she leans her palms on her knees to mimic my pose, and the silence is comfortable. "I have no plans for either a girlfriend or a boyfriend." I nod, the mention of a choice happily raising my eyebrows. "I am enjoying my own sense of place, and right at this moment, with my parent's blessing, I am content to remain there."

"They're okay with that?"

"Oh yes. My parents are free-thinking traditionalists. It makes for interesting conversations in our community."

I don't think either of us is going to eat any more, so I tilt my hand at the chips and she shakes her head. I pull the corners in and bundle up the mess, swivel my body, and stand. The bin is three steps away. When I return, Nyaring is up, holding my bike, and sliding her phone into her pocket.

"Achol says he'll be here in forty minutes. His friend is bringing his ute so we can drop you home first. Your bike will fit in the tray."

"Nyaring, it's okay. I can ride. Seriously."

"No. As I said, my parents expect family to look after family. Family, in my culture, includes those who are friends."

Loads of blinking again. Oh wow. My heart feels almost too large.

"What do you do for Christmas?" she asks.

I shove my hands into my pockets. "We do an orphan's Christmas." Her confused expression makes me smile. "My share house, as you know, has five of us living there, and with the exception of Michelle who goes back to her folks for the holidays, we patch together our own Christmas Day lunch. We get a rotisserie chicken and a pav from the supermarket, and everyone chips in with snags, chops, all the salads, and if we can afford it, a couple of dozen prawns. We do our own drinks. Anyone else we know who's got no-one to be with at Christmas is invited, too. Therefore, orphan's Christmas. The sense of community, whether it's family or found, is something I believe in." I feel shy and proud and vulnerable and strong and maybe Christmas this year will be the moment I truly look forward and not thumb through the photos of regret.

"Do you like to eat, Kate?"

"Um." I point to my solid shape. "Hello?"

She laughs. "Would you like to join my family tomorrow night for Christmas Eve dinner? Afterwards, it is our tradition to gather in the street, and sing hymns as we walk to the church for the service."

I stare. "That…that would be amazing!" I want to hug her, but I've never done that in the whole time we've been friends. So I ask. Her strong arms go over and under mine immediately. It's a brief embrace, but it adds another thread to the tapestry forming in my soul.

She hands me my backpack, and shoulders her own. Then I wrap my left hand over the handlebars.

"Now, my mother is very persuasive so you will not be able to refuse any food." I laugh and she shakes her head, wearing a resigned smile. "No, I'm serious. You'll be offered the first portion, and then it will never end."

Our laughter trails away to the beach.

Naughty or Nice

The ambulance officer walking out to meet us is tall, blonde, feminine in a wearing-a-uniform-but-not-like-a-man way, and perfect for the execs back at the studio. I sigh in resignation, and stick out my hand as she stops in front of us.

"Hi, I'm Caro Petersen, and this is Marta Loriti. Are you Sapphire Kershaw?" We shake hands, Marta delivering the single down-up motion that is her particular quirk, and Sapphire nods.

"Yep. Barry fielded the request and asked me to do the interview. Do you want to go inside or do it out here?"

I defer to Marta, and she contemplates the facade of the ambulance station as a potential backdrop. She takes a step back, her light grey cargo pants sliding over her muscled thighs, then she drops her gaze, and shrugs. Two hands flip over, both shoulders lift, her head tilts to one side, and her mouth turns down for a moment before resuming its position as a horizontal line on her face. The material of the plain white polo shirt moulds itself to her small breasts, her strong shoulders, her biceps, her athletic, gym-created torso. She's breathtaking.

"Here's good," Marta says efficiently. In the year that I've known her, Marta has only ever been efficient. Her speech pattern, her demeanour, her work. All of it efficient. Competent. Strong. Definite. Polite. Smouldering. Mysterious. Sexy. It's a peculiar sensation. One moment, I'm a thirty-three-year-old self-diagnosed straight woman with a much too nice outlook on the world and a much too safe attitude to intimacy, and next minute I'm wildly attracted to a tall, masculine, muscular woman, whose dark eyes undress me, and whose soft olive skin tempts my fingertips.

Marta sets up her silver case, flicking it open so she can sort the LiveU-4G unit, and the laptop. She cradles her Sony HD camera, and I smile. It's her pride and joy, and as a freelance operator, any damage to her equipment means a massive loss of income. I turn to

Sapphire, who is remarkably relaxed and perspiration-free, even in her dark uniform. Meanwhile, I'm sweating in a silk, sleeveless shell top and a business skirt. Possessing pale Nordic skin, and shoulder-length auburn hair means that summer and I are mortal enemies. I pluck out a tissue from my handbag on the ground, and dab lightly at my forehead, cheeks, the hollow of my throat, then between my breasts where the shell top dips a little. My gaze catches Marta's who's handing me the wireless mic. I can tell she's been watching the tissue's journey; a fact which does nothing to halt the perspiration on my skin.

So yes, this year, I questioned my sexuality for the first time. Could I be bisexual? A glance at Sapphire results in not one sexy tingle anywhere in my body. Then, as Marta adjusts the camera, I pause on her quick, nimble fingers, her right thumb adorned with an ornate silver ring, and I nearly burst into flames. It's Marta. As it has been all year.

After a sound test, a final check with my phone screen at my now non-shiny face, and a smile for Sapphire, we're away.

"...a case of people taking care and using common sense," Sapphire says, her voice earnest and compelling, her hands emphasising the words. I know that the majority of the viewers will ignore her Christmas holiday safety message because she's blonde and pretty and a woman, but maybe this year it will get through. I'm optimistic. I ask her about the variety of calls they've received this week, and knowing that Sapphire's face will be filling the frame, I slide my gaze to Marta. She doesn't step outside her metaphorical and physical camera space. She is totally focused. I wonder if she sees me? I want her to see me. I want her to take my hand and lead me to the edge of something. Something other than nice. Something other than safe. I know I could be naughty for her.

"...and the disorientating effects of alcohol, which is a factor in more than forty per cent of drowning deaths. People tend to overestimate their skills but underestimate the risks and therefore get into trouble," Sapphire's clear voice breaks my reverie and I feel the camera refocus.

"Absolutely. Important advice for all of us at Christmas. Thank you for giving us time out of your busy schedule, Sapphire, and thank you for everything you do for our community." I turn slightly. "Back to you in the studio, Candice."

There's a pause, then Marta lowers the camera, and gives me one of her long looks. "It's in the can," she says huskily, then crouches to begin the process of uploading the finished package to the studio for tonight's news bulletin. Her short, shaggy black hair falls forward, and her shirt pulls across her shoulders as she flicks her fingers across the trackpad on the laptop.

"Thanks, Caro," Sapphire says, touching my elbow, and I smile into her startling blue eyes. "Have a great Christmas."

"You, too."

Sapphire, as she turns to leave, delivers the same message to Marta, who looks up, echoes the sentiment, adding a quick smile. I hand the mic to Marta, who stands before taking it from me. Her fingers slide over mine, and I catch my breath. Are colleagues supposed to stand this close? Am I sweating again?

"Do you have anything on for the rest of the evening, Caro?" Marta's low voice fills our space, her dark eyes holding mine.

"No," I say much too quickly.

She smiles, bends to lock the case, then straightens, her head tilted in thought.

"Would you like to grab a drink? You said that you live at Greenway apartments, right?" I nod. She remembers that? "I'm down the block from you at the Twins. Want to meet somewhere in the middle?"

My smile is shy, yet thrilled, which feels odd on my mouth, but must present well because her eyes sparkle.

"Love to," I say. "How about the *King and Crown* on Mitchell Street? Do you know it?"

She does, then she grasps the equipment case, and angles her shoulders to indicate we should walk to the carpark while holding this conversation, which is sensible as it's a billion degrees and our cars have air-conditioning. Marta adjusts her stride to compensate for my heels and smaller stature. She feels incredibly safe. And dangerous. Safely dangerous. I want to experience that safe danger.

A wave of gratitude for our sensible decision to drive to our own apartments, have the world's quickest showers, toss new clothing on, and meet up in an hour rushes over me when I walk into the bar. I'd had enough time to de-gross my body, but not enough to agonise over make-up and clothing choices, or chicken out of the whole invitation altogether. A light-blue dress and sandals, with my hair down, says 'casual drinks', with maybe a hint of 'I want to lick the skin on your throat'. I have no idea what's got into me.

Marta is sitting at a table towards the back, then she stands when I walk towards her. She's in another short-sleeve, white shirt, and light, fawn-coloured pants. We sit as her brief and wonderfully unexpected kiss on my cheek completely disarms me. It's not like I was going in armed anyway, but that gesture has me searching for a white flag. I gather myself, point to the wine menu chalked onto the enormous board on the wall, and ask her to choose.

"I don't drink alcohol, so I think I'll have a club soda with cranberry juice," she says, and I offer to get it, standing before she can change my mind. The couple of minutes I spend at the bar give me time to analyse the concept that alcohol has always sat in the naughty column for me, and finding out that Marta doesn't drink it means throwing away some assumptions. Good. I buy two cranberry juice sodas.

I slide her drink across when I reclaim my seat. We tap glasses.

"Cheers. Merry Christmas," I say.

"Cheers and same." She sips. "Not drinking? But it's—"

"Mm. It's still Christmas." I lift my eyebrows, and she follows their journey with her gaze.

"Okay. So…" she traces lines of condensation on her glass. Good God. "We've worked together off and on all year, and yet this is only the second time we've hung out."

I laugh. "Yes, why is that? Definitely an oversight. I think we…" I pause in thought. "Oh, it was the Food and Wine Festival and we stayed for the rest of the evening with the crew from Channel Four at that Danish Smokehouse."

Marta snorts. "That's right. What was in that smoked sausage you ate?" Then she cracks up at my expression, the lines bracketing her mouth deepening in her tanned skin.

"I have no idea. I don't want to think about it," I say with a full-body shudder.

"You could have said no to the guy," she says, shaking her head slowly, the two small hoops in her left earlobe catching in the light.

"I know. That's my problem. I'm much too nice for my own good."

Marta places her chin in her palm. "You can't say no?"

"No. I mean, I can say no, because I can. But I don't like to make waves. I'm nice…" I fade off and something charges in the air between us. High voltage. My heart jolts, which activates a little stream of consciousness that rushes straight from my mouth. "Don't get me wrong. I'm not a doormat. But all versions of me at the moment encompass the adjectives pleasant and nice. Camera-ready nice. But a darker version of me? I'd like to find her." I sip my drink. Marta hasn't moved. In fact, she hasn't taken her eyes off my face. "Not that there'd be anyone to see Dark 'n Spicy Caro. The only people who watch me with any sort of intensity are camera crew," I lift my eyebrows again, "and that's only because they're being totally professional."

I pause my verbal vomiting, and watch in fascination as Marta's eyes become hooded.

"Not totally," she murmurs.

I blush which, with my skin tone, is basically the setting sun on the foreshore. Marta's lips twitch.

"Well…" I sip my flavoured soda.

"Caro, the camera loves you. Your skin, your hair, your eyes. You look amazing, believe me. I see that. It's pure light. But I can bet that bad Caro is there somewhere."

I don't know what to say, so I fiddle with the coaster under my drink. Marta places her cool fingers over mine. She waits until I make eye contact.

"Do I make you nervous?" Her expression is quizzical, yet knowing.

"Yes, a little." A lot.

"Why? You're not nervous with others. I've seen you. You use your personality, your niceness as you call it, to get what's needed. Look at the paramedic this afternoon. You had her eating out of the palm of our hand."

And in my mind, it's not Sapphire who I see eating anything. It's Marta. Marta eating out of the palm of…any location on my body. My eyes must be revealing some pretty fabulous inner thoughts, because a slow smile develops on her face. I want to tell her that she's been the sole occupant of my dark and stormy thoughts all year. I want to tell her that I burn. She sits back in her seat.

"Should I order a share plate?"

I let out the breath I've clearly been holding. "Yes, please."

The pull of the fabric across her body is delightful to watch, as she saunters to the bar. A washing machine of sensations attacks my stomach. Marta sees me. Has seen me. And now she knows I have a desire to mess with nice Caro and toss a few parts of me into the naughty column. Oh my.

I shift the plastic stand on the table, which advertises the Christmas Day lunch menu, and find a paper checklist underneath. It's clearly a leftover from the lunchtime crowd, as it has been filled in with all sorts of ticks, crosses, and one-word answers. The heading, 'Naughty or Nice: Rate Yourself', leaps out. Marta arrives with a platter of salt and pepper calamari, breads, dips, antipasti, and two side plates.

"What's that?" She tips her chin at the paper.

"I think it's a Christmas quiz that they had for the lunchtime crowd," I say, and I'm about to scrunch it into a ball when Marta's hand folds over mine. She lifts a corner of her mouth at my expression.

"Read one." A bite of calamari disappears into her mouth, and she licks the salt very deliberately from her fingers. We hold our gaze, and I'm aware of the challenge.

"Okay," I say, then I place my own piece of seafood into my mouth and mimic the finger lick. Marta's eyes darken and I feel like I've earned a tick in my shiny new column. I can do this. I smooth the paper out. "Are you naughty or nice if you flipped off more than five people from the safety of your car this year?" I read, and look up as Marta laughs into her chest. I flap the paper. "This is rigged," I moan, which makes her laugh harder.

"You don't flip people off, do you?"

"No! I do swear, though, thank you very much." I point at her amused expression. "Stop it. Are you naughty or nice?"

She smirks. "With that one? Naughty."

I can't help it. "How naughty?"

"Not so naughty." She shrugs, then flicks her fingers, telling me to read another.

"Okay, here. You bought your niece a new recorder for her birthday. Are you naughty or nice?" I scoop some eggplant dip onto my poppyseed flatbread, and chew in contemplation. Marta smiles.

"I don't have a niece."

"Marta…" I huff and she grins, her eyes flashing mischievously.

"Well, it depends." She eats some more food. "A recorder is one of those plastic vertical flute instruments that squeak horrendously and teachers insist on making kids learn, right?"

I nod. "My brother's kids have one each."

"Oh. Well, then it's definitely naughty."

"Why? It's a gift. That's nice," I lean on my elbow, staring at her gorgeous, handsome face.

"Not if you have to listen to the bloody thing," she points out. "You gave your brother's kids something similar for Christmas one year, didn't you?" She bites her lip when I nod. "That was naughty." We laugh, and I mentally slide another tick into my freshly-minted column.

Marta reaches over and spins the paper around.

"All right. This one. Are you naughty or nice if, at the supermarket, you pick a grape and eat it, without actually buying grapes?"

I crack up, rolling my head back on my neck. A delighted sparkle fills her eyes when I let my head fall forward again.

"Oh God, Marta. My mother does that all the time. She says she's testing to see how sweet the grapes are but never buys any." Another tiny giggle pops out. "I belong to the same gene pool, so, yes I've stolen the odd grape or two." I hold up my hand. "Naughty."

Marta leans forward and gently presses her palm to mine in a sort of slow-motion high five. "Guilty as charged," she says quietly. Our hands drop together to the table and she slowly pulls her fingers back, running them over my skin.

Breathing carefully, I lower my gaze to the quiz paper. "Um. So, this one? Are you naughty or nice if you leave one mouthful of milk in the bottle and return it to the fridge so that's all that is available for the next person?" I snap my gaze to hers.

"Irrelevant," we say at the same time, and I laugh.

"Why irrelevant?" Marta asks.

"Single."

"Hmm, Same."

"Oh."

"I guess we're still naughty for that one." Marta gives me another long look, then eats some more of the antipasti and I sip my drink. After a minute, Marta tips her head at me. "How did we score?"

I don't even bother looking at the paper. "I think you're nice," I say and nod once in confirmation. She purses her lips and pulls them to the side. It's rather cute.

"Debatable. We've established that you're incredibly nice." She taps the top of my hand. "Are you ever naughty, besides grape stealing?"

My offended look sends her into another fit of laughter.

"Yes. Of course. My naughty column is growing all the time." I count on my fingers. "I go through the express lane with more than fifteen items. I've had sex on the first date. I jaywalk." Her lips roll in and dimples ping into her cheeks again. "What?"

She laughs. "You are gorgeous, Caro. Firstly, supermarket infringements are not naughty. You're creating traffic flow. Secondly, jaywalking? It's Melbourne. Everyone jaywalks."

I shrug good-naturedly, but hold eye-contact because it's important I see her expression when I make my next point.

"You missed one." I don't recognise the husk in my voice.

"Oh. I did, too. Sex on the first date." She taps her lips. "Probably naughty. But here's the key. Is the sex itself naughty or is it still kind of nice?" The way she says the word 'nice' tells me that nice sex is boring, is unfulfilling, and that the only person getting what they need or want is…not me.

"It's…nice."

There's another long silence.

"So," she places her finger on my hand, slowly drags the tip of it from my knuckle to my nail, and my body shudders. "First date sex that is supposed to be naughty but…isn't?"

"Essentially," I breathe.

"Which means you're nice everywhere," she says, leaning forward, and it feels like I'm magnetised because I lean forward as well.

"I'd rather not be."

"What?"

"Nice everywhere," I murmur, watching her dark eyes narrow.

"Where don't you want to be nice, Caro?"

"You know where." I wrap my hand around her wrist. "I'm…" Newly-forged Naughty Caro waves her hand and shoulders my niceness out of the way. "I'm incredibly attracted to you. You create sparks in me that I desperately need to fan into flames." I breathe. "And I don't know how."

Her smile is wicked, her eyes express an awareness of my need, and her fingers squeeze my hand in acknowledgement of my confusion.

"You don't know how to be…naughty? In the bedroom?" she asks quietly.

I shake my head. "Perhaps..?"

Her lips quirk. "You want me to teach you?"

My breath stops in my throat. "Yes."

She leans even closer. I drop my gaze, and her words are hot near my ear. "I might not be naughty enough."

I tremble. "I think you will be," I say, and look into her eyes.

The connection is extraordinary.

"We're going to need some resources," she says, and a smile ghosts across her lips. "Let's go."

The heat of Marta's hand in the small of my back is burning a hole through the fabric of my dress. I am vibrating with tension. With excitement. We pass a busker who's halfway through 'Deck The Halls' on harmonica and a foot drum. A beret contains a number of coins, and a single five-dollar note. We add to the collection. Then she brings me to a halt at a store, lit brightly, but with the plate glass windows blacked out. *Desires And Dreams* is emblazoned across the facade.

"This is a sex shop," I state, then turn to blink at Marta. She nods seriously.

"Yes." Then the grin she's holding back bursts forth and I can't help responding in kind.

I step into her space.

"What are we doing here?" I ask coyly. I'm having fun.

Marta leans towards my face so that her breath brushes my skin.

"Buying classroom supplies." Her lips touch mine so quickly that I'm sure I only imagined their presence.

As we enter, a floor to ceiling matte-black partition channels both of us to the left, and I realise that the partition acts as a visual barrier for the customers browsing inside and any overt curiosity from the general public on the footpath. The store is a revelation. It's laid out like a supermarket with aisles, signage, bright lighting, display bins of bargains, racks, and two checkouts. I pause in the entrance, embarrassed but eager. I don't quite know what to do—what to say. I glare at myself for being such a nice girl. I'm thirty-three, for heaven's sake. Marta presses into my back and whispers.

"Where do you want to start?"

I have no answer to that question. A young gay couple—at least I assume they're a couple—angles past us, speaking to one of the black T-shirt-wearing sales assistants, the store's logo emblazoned across her chest.

"You know, the red version just came in. It's been such a popular item. Do you want to look at that one?" she asks perkily.

"Absolutely. Does it come with reinforced carabiners?"

I spin and catch Marta unrolling her lips from a smothered smile that is creating dimples in her cheeks again. I grab her hand.

"Help me. You said you'd help."

She raises an eyebrow. "Okay, then. Let's go shopping."

Brad—his name tag announces—appears in front of us as soon as I take a tentative step into the first aisle.

"Can I help you with anything this evening?" He's pleasant, and completely accomodating.

"Oh, um. I'm looking for…" God, what am I looking for? I'm looking for a key. I'm looking for permission. I'm looking for…"A range?" I say, finally. Poor Brad. But his brow furrows thoughtfully, while my brain revs impotently at the starting line. He's giving my clear-as-mud answer serious consideration. Then he delivers a definitive nod, spins on his heel and steps quickly up the aisle to a wall of vibrators.

"So, the bullet vibrator is a classic and perfect for beginners," he says, with a small sweep of his hand, like he's selling drapery on the shopping channel.

"Oh, I have one of those," I announce, squaring my shoulders.

Brad nods once in approval, and Marta's breath drifts across my neck.

"You do? Excellent. Hmm. A little bit naughty," she whispers.

"Oh no. My bullet belongs in the nice category," I murmur, and Marta chuckles quietly. I shiver, softly exhaling my excitement and nerves.

"Well," Brad drags the word out, and takes another step, "You may be interested in one of these. A clitoral vibrator such as this one," he gestures to his right, "and this one," he points to the package hanging above it, "provide powerful suction and stimulation for maximum satisfaction." He sizes us up. "We have a special

Christmas promotion at the moment. If you purchase a second item in this range, you'll receive twenty-five percent off the total."

"Um…" I realise that if I change just a few words in his incredibly calm and objective sales pitch, Brad could be trying to sell me a wrench, or a kitchen appliance. I'm amazed by the entire interaction. However, fluttery tingles still shimmer in my stomach, particularly with Marta pressed so close.

"Those are a little naughty," she murmurs.

"Oh," I say breathily, like a 1950s movie starlet, then I focus on Brad. "I'll take that blue one," I state, pointing at a toy that announces its high-quality air suction capabilities. He beams, flicks the package from the display hook, and thrusts it into my hand.

"I have something else you may like," he says, tossing the words over his shoulder as he bustles off. We trail in his wake. He brings us to a large carousel of jewellery, although when I look more closely, it's not jewellery at all. It's a vast array of clamps. I mean, it could be jewellery, because some of the pieces are quite beautiful, but they're clamps, and…

"Many people find that clamping brings together the pain and pleasure barriers, creating—"

Wild images of skin, and nipples, and sparkly gems on top of silver and leather cloud my mind, and the sharp sting of arousal strikes my core. Marta slides her hand around my waist, and inhales into the hair above my ear.

"They're quite naughty, Caro. I think you should buy a pair."

I clear my throat. "I…I'd like the gold pair with the chain, please, Brad." And just like that, two checkmarks appear on my Christmas naughty list. I break out in goosebumps, and Marta's soft chuckle only adds to their permanency on my skin.

Brad appears in front of me. I hadn't seen him leave. Before I realise, he's taken the items from my hand, dropped them into a plastic grocery basket. He passes it to me, I grasp the black double handles, and juvenile giggles threaten because I really could be in aisle five of *BargainBuy* selecting rice noodles. My giggles dissolve when he holds up a pair of pink faux-leather handcuffs.

"These are very popular and have received some outstanding reviews from our customers."

My nodding, a simple gesture to indicate that I'm listening, is interpreted as a desire to purchase, because Brad places the pink handcuffs into the red basket. I turn to stare at Marta, who winks—swoon—and she mouths the words "very naughty". Brad states that he has other items for us to view, so we accompany him further into the store. He pauses at the boxes of Japanese ropes, tilts his head in thought, flicks his gaze to me, then delivers a soft grunt, seeming to dismiss the idea he may have had. I breathe a sigh of…relief? Then I look up. There is an entire floor to ceiling display of whips, and paddles, and I spin to stare at Marta. Her eyes are dark as she returns my gaze. "Yes," she whispers.

"This is one of our most popular whips," Brad says. I jerk my attention back, and he places one of those popular whips into my hands. It's purple, and sports a tag stating that it's fifty-six centimetres of pure leather. My fingers absently roll the individual strands, and I catch Marta's eyes following the movements. Liquid heat builds between my thighs.

"I think…I think that's everything I need," I say, and Brad smiles, seemingly thrilled that he's been able to assist with my purchases. We make our way to the checkout, the normality of the experience still throwing me off a little. Brad rings up the purchases, dropping each item into a plain cloth recycled bag, then as I pluck out my credit card, he slides in a packet of dams and a tube of lubricant. I stutter, then smile, because that's sensible, and excellent service, and oh gosh, I want to hurry home—my place? I hope so. I need to play. I'm ready to jump columns and frolic in the naughty.

With the handles joined together, Brad passes the bag across and wishes us a Merry Christmas, and suddenly we're on the footpath, staring at each other's smiles.

Marta places her hands on my waist, holding me close. "Your place?" she asks, and I breathe out.

"Yes."

The lock on my apartment door proves to be rather recalcitrant, as the key trembles in my hand. Then we're inside, and Marta pushes me up against the inside of the door.

"I have wanted to do this for so long, Caro," she whispers near my cheek, my ear, my hair, chasing the words with soft kisses. She cradles my breasts, thumbs teasing, then slides one hand down to cup me, pushing the fabric of my dress into my centre. I jerk with arousal. She steps back, and I realise that I'm still clutching the bag. I hold it out.

"Oh no," Marta laughs. "You hang onto that. Opening the packaging is part of the fun. Once you do that, then we'll play in whatever column you like."

"I'm…some of these things…it seems like a lot for just one night…to use on one person."

I breathe shallowly as she carefully unbuttons her shirt, shrugs it from her torso, then flicks off her bra to reveal the top half of her muscled, tanned, delectable body. My eyes linger.

"Caro," she purrs. "Who says this is a short lesson? Who says that those," her eyebrow quirks, "are just for you?"

I hold her gaze, the bag hanging loosely from my fingers.

Marta licks her lips. "So…the question is" she smiles crookedly. "Naughty?" She drags a finger down the middle of her chest. "Or nice?"

My smile is slow. "Ohhh, that's very nice."

Unexpected Gifts

Christmas Eve at Laskin Beach is quite delightful. It's crowded and I need to watch my step, but everyone is bubbling and fizzing with the kind of excitement that only the day before Christmas can bring. The wide footpath—they call it a boardwalk nowadays—is lined with stalls filled with extraordinary artwork, craft, products, and promotions. I can remember when the Laskin Markets consisted of ten stalls, each selling knock-off cassettes of the latest rock band, or handmade clothing. It's now a tourist attraction in its own right, and accents from all around the world fill my ears. A smile stretches my mouth.

I can remember when roller-blading started to become popular just after Syl and I moved to our little cottage three streets back from the beach. The footpaths were clearer then, and the gorgeous women zigging and zagging forwards and backwards along the foreshore always held my attention. Syl laughed and called me an old perv, but I always noticed her having a bit of a look as well. I cracked another joke about checking out women just the other night.

Nowadays, the baby strollers outnumber the rollerblades. I don't think rollerblades are 'in' anymore, so to speak. But the mums, some clearly lesbian couples, are out in force this afternoon. Laney says I need to use the proper terminology.

"It's not lesbian, Mum. It's queer," she mutters every time I talk about Syl and I or couples we know. I always forget, but I try to practice. I nod at two women—queer women—as they stroll past the stall that sells the beautiful landscape paintings, and I receive a nod in return. I must tell Syl that I haven't lost my gaydar, and that the lesbian head nod is still in fashion. I'll make sure Laney doesn't hear that.

Across the way is the photographer's stall. Now there's a lesbian. I know she is, because it came up in conversation when Syl and I were scouring the markets last year for a birthday present for Ollie.

We'd found the perfect gift; a hand-turned wooden bowl, and then spent some time stopping at the other stalls to chat. The photographer has an unusual name. It's something short. I can't quite recall, which is becoming a common occurrence lately. Rather frustrating. But I remember her smile lighting up when she discovered that old lesbian couples exist in the wild. Syl teased her —Zed, that's her name—about the comment and we laughed. She's helping a customer, so I give her a wave, and get a beaming smile in return.

Zed is trying something new this year. She's using the rollercoaster as a backdrop. That rollercoaster holds a special place for Syl and me. We met while waiting in line. I was there with a couple of mates to celebrate Andy's birthday. It was strange visiting a theme park for a thirtieth birthday party, but Andy was into nostalgia and it was a bit of a lark. So there we were, in our acid-washed jeans, tennis shoes, over-sized T-shirts. I even had leg-warmers on. Talk about the height of fashion. Well, it was 1981. Andy was bopping about to the music blaring from the speakers near the entrance when he barrelled into me. I stumbled forward into the woman in front, and when she turned, I fell again. Right into her blue eyes. Oh my. Hair full of long curls that had been teased out so they hung about her head like a halo. A denim jacket, covered in patches promoting bands, causes, solidarity, and on the upper-right sleeve, a rainbow flag. I didn't realise then, but Syl was one of the first in Melbourne to wear the flag. It had only been out in society since 1978. That fact makes me proud. We started dating pretty much straight away, although we had to be subtle. Neither of us was out to our families, and the world still wasn't overly friendly to lesbians. Not in the 1980s in Melbourne. But we'd meet at the beach, and go for walks. And talk. I think that's why Syl insisted we buy a house here. Because of the memories.

The stall that is four down from Zed's sells movie memorabilia, and the poster on display at the front makes me chuckle. It's of Mad Max 2, which is the film I took Syl to as one of our first dates. I still don't know what I was thinking. Syl always slides it into conversations at dinner with Laney and Ollie and the grandkids, and we all get a good laugh at my inept attempts to woo my new girlfriend. Luckily, the walks along Laskin Beach saved me.

We've all been that new. New to ourselves. New to others. I guess that's why I love seeing the newness of lesbian relationships, like the one I'm positive I've seen starting between the shy butch manager at *Bargain Buy* and the customer who's been trying to hide her attraction. It was certainly something to tell Syl about on Tuesday night because the woman resembled Syl so closely. Syl, with her gorgeous curves and her light brown hair, captured my heart the day we met. Still does. I didn't see the customer's eyes but I like to think they are the same blue as Syl's. The blue of the sky when the sun is at its peak in summer and you look at the patch just above the horizon line. That blue.

The blue that's falling from the sky right now on this little section of Melbourne. It was a very gay suburb when we moved here, and it has stayed the same ever since. Just one of those funny quirks that happen in cities where all the gays—"Queer, Mum!"—tend to congregate in one or two locations. Now, the rainbow flags outnumber the Australian flags, and here at the Christmas market, there's a rainbow flag vying for position next to every piece of limp tinsel.

It's a very validating sight. We worked so hard over the years to be accepted. When Syl and I bought our house, we had to fight tooth and nail for a bank loan. Not being married was a huge stumbling block, which is why we joined the protest march that wound through the beachside streets during the marriage equality debate. It was only a few years ago, and both of us were slower and older and found the distance and intensity of the march a bit much. But we did it. The government passing the marriage equality legislation into law right before Christmas that year was the best present we could have received. Syl and I got married on Laskin Beach the following year. We were barefoot, and it was perfect.

I was laughing with Syl the other night as I thumbed through some of the wedding photos. My big goofy grin stars in so many of them. Syl, of course, looks stunning, although on the day, I found her having a bit of a cry in the bedroom.

"What's up, love?" I'd said, holding her to my chest.

"I'm too old, Nola. I'm not that young lass you knocked over at the fairground. I look silly all dressed up like this." She was so sad, but I told her how much I love her and what an amazing life we have and how gorgeous she is. I reminded her of how many Christmases we'd had together. Christmas is Syl's number one absolute favourite celebration. That coaxed a smile from her.

Our wedding photos are probably still scattered on the dining table from the other night. I should tidy them up. One of the photos in particular makes my breath catch. Syl's leaning over the railing on the little verandah at the front of our house. She's staring at me, smouldering, and I pointed it out to her last night, because that reporter on the local news had the same look. I don't think those looks, from the reporter or Syl, are ever consciously created. I reckon it's innocent until they see someone they desire, and then it's like they're going to devour that person. It's intoxicating. I hope whoever that reporter was looking at or thinking about understood the level of sexy focus they were receiving. And was going to do something about it.

My wanderings take me past the amazing, imposing, brand new lifeguard tower. What a huge effort that was! Petitioning the council to finally supply a tower that supported the safety requirements of a beach like Laskin. Every year, it seems more and more people are flocking here for the Christmas period, and making some really poor decisions. Just like that ambo was saying on the TV last night.

I notice that they're setting up the speakers and equipment for the *Carols By Candlelight* in the little park that sits cosily in the bend of Beach Road. There are *Carols By Candlelight* events all over Melbourne tonight; the big one in town is at the Botanic Gardens. But we love the local one. There's usually a celebrity or two who can hold a tune, and Santa turns up for the kids. It's a lovely event. Another of Syl's favourites. A large banner announces the celebrity for tonight, and it's the actor from a popular Channel Four TV drama. I must tell Syl about it when I get home. I pause at the rock wall, and contemplate sitting, but I know I'll have a hard time getting going again. I enjoy my walks but some days it takes just a little longer. I think, at Christmas, I take longer on purpose.

Seeing Frank being carted off by those fabulously competent women ambos yesterday was a bit of a shock. I mean, it wasn't because he's always calling for the ambulance, but each time I see it happen, I wonder if it's his last ride. Goodness, he's only ten years younger than I am, and I don't see seventy as that old. Not if I'm still able to walk the two kilometres to *Bargain Buy* every second day. Laney started on about it last year.

"Mum, why are you and Mumma still walking to get groceries? Surely you can take your car and get them once a week like everyone else?"

Explaining the idea of community connection to our daughter made Syl and I laugh ironically, because Laney and Ollie live in one of those gated communities over the other side of Melbourne. They're actually designed to foster community. But our little cottage is perfect. Just right in size, and handy to the markets, and other amenities.

Speaking of Laney, it is inconceivable that she's forty this year. Syl said a while back that it meant we were getting old, then she laughed, and did that flirtatious shoulder wriggle and I kissed her, holding her against me at the kitchen wall. Gosh, if we could have created a child from our lovemaking, we would have, but Laney was the result of Greg, our longtime friend, depositing his sperm into a turkey baster, Syl lying flat on her back and me providing the encouragement for the little swimmers as I squeezed the tube. It worked, though. Oh my, our parents were upset. Loads of pearl-clutching and threats to disown us eventually carried out. Syl and I tried not to care. I still get sad that Laney didn't get to know her grandparents. Makes me cry a little, although only in front of Syl. She always said our Christmases would have been just a bit…more if they'd changed their views.

So we have done Chosen Family Christmases ever since Laney was born. Chosen family, such as longtime friends who are like aunts and uncles to Laney, and Ollie's parents who are fabulous and who we love to bits. The grandkids, Lee and Nick, are two cheeky monkeys at ten and eight years of age.

I wish Syl had joined me on my market wanderings today, but it's not to be. Thinking about her waiting at home puts a burst of energy into my steps.

After a while, I turn into our street. The sun has a burnt tinge now, like it always gets around six or seven o'clock during summer. Like the furnace is shutting down and the evening cool comes knocking. The white gate in our front fence sticks a little, and I make a note to have a go at fixing it on Boxing Day. I might have to ask Ollie, though. My hands aren't strong enough sometimes.

My key slips into the front door lock, and I push inside.

"Hello, love. I'm home," I call, and bustle into the kitchen. It's a comfortable little space with a tiny dining table, just perfect for two, and the small lounge room only a step away with a fireplace, and chairs and a TV. I'm making Syl's favourite tonight; roast lamb and veggies, although I'm cheating a bit because I picked up a pre-cooked version at *Bargain Buy* yesterday so all I have to do is pop it into the microwave. But not yet. The unopened whiskey bottle, a gift from Philippa at the animal shelter where I volunteer, beckons me, so I take down one of Syl's cut-glass tumblers, crack the seal, and draw out a tray of ice cubes from the freezer. My thumbs don't like pushing on the back of the tray but finally two fall out, and I flick them into my glass. Then, with a couple of fingers of the lovely amber liquid over the ice, I take the glass and sag into my armchair in the lounge room. My chair is directly under the ceiling fan; a Godsend on days like today. The breeze ruffling my hair reminds me that I've still got to wrap the grandkid's presents tonight. Wrapping Christmas presents in summer is to leap into battle against the wind buffeting down from ceiling fans, while avoiding touching the paper with your sweaty hands. It should be an Olympic event.

"I'll just have this drink, love, then dinner. Then I'll pop down to the Carols." I stare at the dormant fireplace. "I'll light a candle, sweetheart and sing a bit, even though you always said I sound like a bullfrog." I swallow a mouthful of the whiskey around the lump in my throat. The beautifully carved Tasmanian oak box sits quietly on the mantlepiece. Syl's ashes are inside. She always liked the smell of the oak from Australia's island state. We never visited, but she'd stood at the woodturning stall at the Christmas market a few years back, picked up the box and stuck her nose to the lid, breathing deeply. Her smile was brighter than the sun that December. She'd bought the box and when she left me last January, she made me promise to keep it because it smelled like Christmas.

"You got your wish, sweetheart," I whisper. "I keep my promises. Like the one I made to you to get out of the house and do things. I've been doing that. I can just see your expression if you found out I'd been sitting inside all day."

My laugh is quick and singular.

"There's so much life out there, but I feel so bloody guilty, going out and about, living life, seeing life, watching all the fresh beginnings." My throat is tight again. "But they're delightful to see. You'd have loved the cute couple I told you about the other night. So nervous. So new."

Tears fill my eyes, and I shake my head to help blink them away. The first Christmas without my Sylvia. Another sip of whiskey soothes the burn of sadness that rises again. I contemplate the box. I like knowing her spirit is free of a body overtaken with illness. The cancer took Syl. No. Syl left with the cancer. She left. But she made sure she stayed long enough to say goodbye. She stayed long enough for one more Christmas. Syl told me it was because she wanted to make sure that I knew how much she loved me.

"I knew, sweetheart."

The ice cubes have melted. Not surprising.

"Laney and Ollie are picking me up tomorrow for Christmas lunch at their place. They've had their new pool put in, and you just know that Lee and Nick will be in it all day. I imagine we'll spend most of the afternoon outside."

I stare into the glass.

"I had a word with Laney last week. She was worrying about my mental health of all things. Worried that I'd hide away." I chuckle. "I said that my grief is mobile, and if I choose to take it with me when I'm out and about, then I'll do so."

The little Christmas tree—only a metre in height—sits in the corner of the lounge. It's made of plastic, which Syl and I agreed was sensible, because a real tree in an Australian summer is bonkers. I've tossed some tinsel over it, and plonked the star on top, but I couldn't bring myself to unwind the fairy lights from the box in the cupboard. I think that might have been the last straw. Too many emotions wrapped up in those infernal things.

"Merry Christmas, love." I raise my glass. "I imagine you're up there perving on all the ladies. Hope they're wearing tinsel and not much else."

Our love was big, and full, and Syl taught me that every day is special. Not just Christmas Day. She always said that scattered throughout each day are little gifts. You just had to find them. And cherish them. Those unexpected gifts.

The End

I sincerely hope you enjoyed reading *An Unexpected Gift*. If you did, I would greatly appreciate a review on your favourite book website. Or even a recommendation in your favourite lesbian fiction Facebook group. Reviews and recommendations are crucial for any author, and even just a line or two can make a huge difference. Thanks!

About the author

Best-selling author KJ lives in Melbourne, Australia with her wife, their son, three cats and a dog. Her novel, Coming Home, was a Goldie finalist. Her other best-selling novels include Learning To Swim, Kick Back, and Art of Magic.

Twitter at @propertyofkj
Instagram at kjlesfic
Facebook at www.facebook.com/kj.lesfic.7/

Subscribe to my newsletter
https://tinyletter.com/KJauthor

Printed in Great Britain
by Amazon